THE FLOOD

David Maine

CANONGATE

Edinburgh · New York · Melbourne

Published in 2004 as THE PRESERVATIONIST by
St. Martin's Press in the United States of America

First published in Great Britain in 2004 by
Canongate Books Ltd, 14 High Street,
Edinburgh EH1 1TE

This edition published by Canongate in 2005

10 9 8 7 6 5 4 3 2 1

British Library Cataloguing-in-Publication Data
A catalogue record for this book is available
on request from the British Library

1 84195 630 9

Typeset in Janson Text 11/15 by
Palimpsest Book Production Limited, Polmont, Stirlingshire
Printed and bound in Great Britain by
Clays Ltd, St Ives plc
Book Design by James Hutcheson

www.canongate.net

for Uzee

AUTHOR'S NOTE

Quotations are taken from the 1914 printing of the
Douay Bible, translated by the English College at
Rheims in 1582 and first published at Douay in 1609.
All names are spelled as in that edition.

PART ONE
CLOUDS

I
Noe

But Noe found grace before the Lord.
GENESIS 6:8

Noe glances toward the heavens, something he does a lot
these days. Scanning for clouds. None visible amid the
stars, so he finishes urinating, shakes himself dry and makes
his way back to the house. Inside, the wife pokes desul-
torily at a pot of stew hanging over a fire. It is late for
supper: the others have eaten already and retired to the
sleeping room. Noe squats against one of the rough limewashed walls and points at a terracotta bowl. He's roughly
six hundred years old: words are unnecessary.

The stew is thick with lentils and goat. Noe slurps
contentedly. A little salt would improve it, but salt is in
short supply of late.

Noe finishes the stew, sets the bowl aside, clears his
throat. The wife recognizes this as a signal of forthcoming
speech and offers her attention. Noe says, I must build a
boat.

—A boat, she says.

—A ship, more like. I'll need the boys to help, he
adds as an afterthought.

3

The wife squats on the far side of the fire, paddle-like feet set wide apart, forearms poised on knees. She fiddles with the wooden ladle and says, You know nothing much of boats. Or ships either.

—I know what I need, he says.

—We're leagues from the sea, she says, or any river big enough to warrant a boat.

This conversation is making Noe impatient.—I've no need to explain myself to you.

She nods. The olive-oil lamp throws a soft yellow glow across them both. The wife is sturdily built, short and broad, and much younger than Noe: perhaps sixty. She was barely adolescent when wed to the old man, already white-bearded to his navel, with crow's-feet sunk into his temples like irrigation ditches. Still a vital old corker, though, and randy enough to rut her into three sons. Nowadays a stranger would have trouble guessing which of them was the senior.

—And when you're done, she says carefully, we'll be taking this ship to the sea somehow?

As usual, Noe's impatience fades quickly.—We'll not be going to the sea. The sea will be coming to us.

She's banked the fire and taken the pot off already, but stirs it now out of habit. Her fingers are long and tapering.—It's one of your visions?

—Yes, Noe says quietly.

There is a pause.

—So that's it then, she says.

The wife looks up with a sad smile. For a moment she appears thirteen again, fourteen, and Noe glimpses the oval-faced girl half-hidden behind her brothers, eyes down, brought out to the front yard for his approval before he took her away on his mule. Something stirs in him then, simple and tender, and briefly he is regretful for all the anxiety he knows she will face. But it can't be helped. He has been called. More than that: he has been chosen, and there is something he must do.

The wife says, I guess you'd better get started.

—I guess I'd better, Noe agrees. But there is a small sad glitter in his wife's eyes, and he looks away while he speaks.

This is what happened when Noe received the vision.

He was in the mustard field, yellow flowers in all directions so bright they seared his corneas. Zephyrs ruffled them like silks on a line, like the surface of a pond. Dazzled by the shimmer, Noe strode through the patch, walking staff clutched in his gnarled right hand. His mind was busy with thoughts of trade, of what he could get from Dinar the peddler in exchange for a few hundredweight of mustard greens, of olives from his grove, of goat's milk and hen's eggs and sheep's wool. Some wine, perhaps, to fend off the midwinter dankness; or a few bolts of eastern cloth; or some salt, yes, definitely some salt. Doubtless the wife would have suggestions too, a copper pot, a better loom. Always there was something. Thank Yahweh he had no daughters to marry off and no dowries to accumulate.

He heard the bleat of a lamb nearby. The sheep were supposed to be far to the east, on the hillsides with Japheth. Had one strayed?

—*Noe.*

The voice did not come from outside his head so much as inside. He staggered, but kept walking.

—*Noe.*

His hands were pressing against his forehead without his knowing it.—Who—?

—*Noe.* He felt a physical pressure behind his temples, a gentle swelling against the inside of his skull. Though disconcerting, it felt in no way alarming.—*I am here.*

—Yes Lord, he managed to stammer.

—*Noe, you are a good man. There are few such.*

Noe said nothing.

—*I am pleased with you and your sons. There are many I am not pleased with. Do you understand what I am saying?*

—Not exactly, my Lord.

—*The unbelievers shall be destroyed.*

Little more than a whisper:—Destroyed?

—*They shall be drowned in a flood of righteousness and brought before Me for judgment.*

Noe felt his bladder loosen, and hot urine streamed down his thigh.—As you wish, Lord. I pray that you will look with mercy upon my sons and myself, though we deserve it not.

—*Fear not, Noe. I have plans for you.*

Noe had long since stopped walking. Around him the hallucinatory vision of burning golden flowers filled his eyes with tears.

—*You are going to build a boat, Noe. Not just any boat. Something enormous, hundreds of cubits, big enough for you and your family and their families. Do you understand?*

6

—Yes, Lord.

—*When it is complete, you will collect every animal you can account for, male and female, as many as possible. Put them on this boat, and provision it well, because you know not how long you will be afloat. There will be a deluge.*

—I'll do as you instruct.

—*When the rain stops, you and your families and the animals you save shall go forth and fill the land again. All else shall perish.*

Noe nodded. It was either that or fall over. If he hadn't pissed himself already, he would do so now.—Lord, about this vessel.

—*Make it big*, advised Yahweh.

—A hundred cubits?

—*Three hundred. Fifty wide, and thirty tall. With three decks, and tar inside and out, and a pair of doors set into the side tall enough for three men.*

Despair chewed through him like a maggot.—My Lord, that is immense indeed. It will take time. And wood, he thought to himself, but didn't say aloud.

Not that it mattered.—*Time I will give. And timber others will bring you, if you but have faith enough.* And then Yahweh, the Lord God of Noe's ancestor Adam and Adam's son Seth, evaporated from Noe's mind.

—Lord?

No answer. Noe's thoughts alone were present in Noe's head. He blinked. Tears tracked down his face and dry urine tugged stickily among the hairs on his calf. The sun toiled down relentlessly, reflected back by a thousand thousand tiny mustard blossoms. In their midst stood a dirty gray-white smudge: one of Noe's lambs, far astray and bleating furiously.

Noe took this as a sign. He took many things as signs. He rushed the lamb, who stood riveted as if too startled to jump away. The old man scooped the animal and murmured, You're coming with me. You'll be the first.

—Baa, answered the lamb.

With purpose now, Noe made for the farm buildings, square whitewashed things like cubes of dirty chalk in the distance. His bony, bowed legs pumped vigorously, belying his great age. Noe knew that great age was not an obstacle to great deeds. Fatigue could be overcome; stiffness could be chased away. Forgetfulness could be managed or even turned to one's own advantage. Yahweh's words rattled in his ears as he hurried on.

If you but have faith enough.

2
The wife

*And Noe, when he was five hundred years old, begot
Sem, Cham, and Japheth.*

GENESIS 5:31

So when Himself starts with the visions and the holy
labors and the boat full of critters, what am I supposed to
do? Talk sense? Ask questions he can't answer, like, How
do you propose to keep the lions from eating the goats?
Or us for that matter?

No thanks. I just fuss with the stew and keep my
thoughts stitched up in my head where they belong. Long
ago I quit asking questions. A person learns fast that with
Himself, there's not a lot in the way of conversation. He
talks, proclaims, pontificates; other people nod. That's how
he likes it. Does he even know my name? Don't bet on it.
It's been years now, decades, since I've heard anyone speak
it, least of all him. I'm the wife now, no more, no less.

I can even pinpoint the day I gave up trying to change
this. It was on the ride here, the afternoon of our nuptial
feast in fact. I'd been the wife since mid-morning; I'm
nothing if not a quick study.

The day I left my father's holding for good, forty-odd

years ago, I rode sidesaddle on a mule behind the old man who was, by repute, on the far side of five hundred. Mule didn't look a lot younger. I didn't mind; I was ready for some adventure, which should give an idea of just how empty my head was back then.

Himself was a novelty all right. Lizard skin and hands like roots. Big cloud of hair like a patch of uncut wool dragged through the dust a few dozen times. About the only thing with sharp edges were his eyes, blue like thick ice, only I didn't know that then, never having seen thick ice up to that point. Or thin ice either. They could snap onto you and choke you off mid-sentence. Or they did me, anyway. At first I tried asking him things on that ride home. I was only a girl, after all, and had never seen him before. Knew his reputation, of course. Everyone knew about ageless Noe. Some said he was a devil, but most said he was touched by Yahweh. Grandson of Mathusala, himself grandson to Jared; the whole lot of them able to trace their ancestors back a thousand years to Adam himself, to Eden and the Fall. But then that wasn't so special in those days; plenty of folks could do it. My pa could do that himself, or so he claimed.

Jared and Mathusala, though, that was something. Talk about a well-connected family. My pa was thrilled, simple man that he was. Poor as dust, with no dowry to speak of, and here's Noe saying he didn't care. Saying my pa's virtuous lifestyle and my own modest purity were treasures more valuable than any property. Pa laughed for two months straight about that, then had a big feast and got me onto that mule pronto, before the old man could change his mind.

Don't let me give the wrong impression; I *was* modest, and pure as any thirteen-year-old could be who'd started her cycles and woke up wet from time to time in the middle of the night. And my pa was virtuous, in a sort of hopeless, no-point-being-otherwise kind of way. What tickled him was the idea that he should be given credit for habits that he had fallen into more or less by chance.

So there we are on the mule, saddlebags clanking, leather whining and my backside all but worn off from the old man's threadbare excuse for a riding blanket, which I'm thinking probably predates old Mathusala himself. It's no boast to say I had a pretty fair backside in those days, too, but everything changes as we all know. At this point my pa's land has long since faded into the horizon and I'm starting to wonder, Now what? It's late afternoon, the sun low in the west like a melon, the land flat and parched and none too promising. My pa's land was bad enough, but this. A straggling line of hills to the north seems to be where we're headed, but in the meantime there's little to distinguish one spot from the next. A few scrubby bushes, some thorny, sticklike trees, the odd hillock. Snake holes underfoot and buzzards lazing on the updrafts.

—How much further? I ask, by way of conversation. —Will we be there by nightfall?

No answer. Not even a shake of the head or a sigh. I'm thinking, He's old, maybe the hearing's not so good.

In fact I'm in no hurry. We're due for a full moon, and somehow the notion of riding to my new life in its pale silvery light, safe behind the shoulders of this man calling himself my husband, gives me a little trill that ripples right down my back into my hips. I shift on the mule's bony spine.

Still, I'm curious. So a little louder, I lean toward him and say, Will we be there before dark?

Without turning he snaps his hand back across my face.

The awkward angle saves me; his fingers catch my chin and nose but not with any great force. Still the meanness of it is a shock. In thirteen years my pa has never laid a hand on me in anger. Tears boil up. I gasp, catch my breath, lose it again.—Turn around, I gag.—Turn around right now and take me home.

The mule stops. Himself faces me over his shoulder, eyes glittering with flat orange melonlight.—That's what I'm doing, he says.—Taking you home.

My breathing is deep and unsteady.

—Four centuries I've been alone, he says.—I've lived with no parents or brothers or in-laws. I'm a man of settled habits. I'm not accustomed to children yelling in my ear and I'll not get used to it now. That's clear then?

When I bite the inside of my cheek, hard, the pain gives me something to hold on to so as not to cry. He apparently takes my silence for assent, for he says, Good, and kicks the mule into motion.

I remember thinking, Maybe this is what Hell is like.

I also remember thinking: He kicked the mule about as hard as he hit me. Not so as to hurt it; just enough to make sure it obeyed.

The moon is well up when we stop next. I've pretty well moved beyond any notions of romantically riding into the future behind the noble figure of my new protector, and I'm glad enough to rest.

We've stopped in a patch of arid desolation unremarkable from the larger desolation we've been riding through. He unties the blanket from the mule's back and spreads it on the ground, making a point of clearing away the thorny brush and some of the larger stones. This softens me a little toward him, though mostly I'm just exhausted. I wouldn't say no to a meal but one doesn't seem forthcoming.

—Think you'll be comfortable here? he asks.

I want to say, I've slept on the ground all my life, what do you take me for? But I don't want to sound petulant. Instead I lie down, cover my eyes with my arm, and wonder when things start to get better.—Of course.

—Roll over then.

I'm already half-asleep, so I just murmur, Mmm?

—On your stomach, girl.

I move my arm then and look. And wouldn't you know, the old man's got himself ready like a stud bull.—Good God, I say, unable to contain myself.

—True enough, he says, and leans down to pat my hip.—You're a farm girl, you know how this works.

So I do, but it's no use. I've gone dry as ashes and I can't take my eyes off that wagging cactus, as big as my two fists stacked one on the next. As much to get rid of the sight as anything else, I roll onto my belly, feel him fumble with the hem of my riding tunic, hiking it up around my waist. Then his leathery fingers pull at my hips, an awkward angle that grinds my chin into the blanket. Mule stink in my nose as he pushes against my spot, but even he can tell this isn't working.

—It's not my aim to hurt you, he says after a time.

—Then stop.

He does, sighing so hard that the wind whistles through his nostrils. There's some rawness between my legs, then the warm rough clutch of his hand squeezing my backside.—Well, I've waited this long, a little more won't kill me.

—Thank you, I whisper, thinking, A little more of this might kill *me*.—I'm just so tired. Later will probably be okay.

He lets the hem of his tunic drop back to his knees. —You let me know, wife. I'll be ready.

I bet you will is what I think, but I keep it to myself.

And later, sometime before dawn, I wake to a presence on my thigh and a heaviness elsewhere. The presence is his hand. The heaviness is inside of me. I shift, and the hand moves but doesn't leave.

—Well? he says.

I roll over and hoist myself into the air.—Try.

He needs no encouragement. He splays my legs and fumbles into me, and it's as though I don't have time to dry up. There is pain, yes, when he shoves through, a brief hot tearing followed by a dull ache, like pressing a bruise again and again, but there's some kind of excitement too, almost pleasure. Though nothing, apparently, compared to what Himself is feeling. The way he carries on, I expect to be a widow by morning. Grunts give way to moans and then strangled shrieks, as if the old boy's being eaten by ants. When it's over he collapses beside me, his tunic still clumped round his stomach.

In the morning he ruts me again before demanding breakfast. I dig out some hard traveling biscuits from the saddlebags and try to ignore the pain. We sit and eat, him barely meeting my eye. Just before we ride off he catches my arm and says, That didn't hurt now, did it?

—Some, I tell him.

He looks away as if befuddled. Clearly this wasn't the answer he wanted. That night we sleep out again after another day on the mule riding through nothing much. Those mountains to the north slide by on our right and still we plod on. Dinner is olives and apricots and crumbling goat cheese. He takes me again of course, quicker this time and harder. If anything it hurts more, the raw wound being stretched. But when he asks me again, before dozing off, That didn't hurt this time, did it? I remember the morning and say, No, husband, not at all.

That seems to relieve him. Seems to assure him that after all these years he's done the wise thing and gotten himself a normal wife. Praise God. He mumbles something and falls asleep in moments, leaving me to spend the night staring at the pale dried milkstain of stars spilling across the sky like a ghostly memory. Like something once bright and new that has worn over time and faded and become dull.

3
Noe

Now giants were upon the earth in those days.

GENESIS 6:4

Noe says to his eldest son: I must go away for a time.

—All right, says Sem.

—I need you to go to the coast and bring Cham. Japheth can manage the farm.

—Yes Father, says Sem.

Japheth snickers and is ignored.

Cham has been learning the shipbuilding trade for four years. Noe had thought this was expediency. Now he realizes it was Providence.

—He must bring his wife as well, and any children they may have.

—Yes Father.

—Yes Father, Japheth singsongs mockingly. Mirn, his wife, pokes him. He pokes her back.

—Japheth, that's enough, says Noe's wife. Japheth smirks and finishes his bread, says to Mirn, Come on, we've work to do outside. But instead of going out, they return to the sleeping room. Noe sighs. His youngest is still a child, with a gangly sixteen-year-old's body full of a sixteen-year-old's desires. And a fourteen-year-old wife who looks like a boy herself.

To Sem he says, If they ask questions, tell them nothing. Tell them it is my wish that they come. Tell them, if you must, that I am dying.

—Yes Father.

Noe hesitates. He has just given his son three contradictory instructions, and Sem has assented to them all. If pressed, he would acknowledge no conflict. But what does Noe expect? Sem is the good son, the one who never grumbles like Cham or smirks like Japheth. Sem's imagination is as square and dull as his hands, his character as stolid and thickset as his midriff. Sem is the one who always obeys. For many years this has brought joy to Noe's heart. Fruit of his loins and so on. At the moment he's not so sure. There will be hardship ahead: perhaps a bit of independent thinking might be called for.

Sem interrupts his thoughts.

—Anything else, Father?

—No no, go on.

Sem rises to leave. The family has been gathered in the main room, eating breakfast. Ants hurry to collect crumbs. Outside the hint of sunrise smears the sky over the low hills. Sem's wife Bera rises also but Noe lifts a hand.—Wait.

She waits. In the other room Japheth grunts sharply, then falls silent.

—Your father. You've not seen him lately?

An absurd question. Bera stares speechless and Noe well knows why. She hasn't seen her father since age seven,

17

when he traded her as part of the ransom for prisoners of war. This in one of the southern kingdoms. Her father was the headman of his tribe, blessed with thirty wives and a hundred children, and had eagerly swapped virgins for warriors.

At fifteen, aged much past her years, Bera entered service in the home of a wealthy Canaanite trader, a widower who followed the faith of Adam, already at that time being forgotten by many. This trader had taught her the rudiments of the faith—they were simple enough—and then died.

What, then, had led the peddler Dinar to take her on his dray into the remote northern territories, where he'd heard that Noe sought a wife for his firstborn? Chance, many would say. Luck as blind as a leech. But to Noe, who saw the finger of God in every ripple of water and His wrath in every hornet's sting, Dinar's arrival with the wide-eyed girl of uncertain provenance but undeniable physical assets—and Sem's willingness to go along with this, as with every instruction from his father—amounted to no less than a direct order from Yahweh Himself. To refuse this bounty would be to spit in God's eye, never a good idea.

So Noe bought the girl and gave her to his son and had them married. She gave her name as Bera and offered little else, but settled in quickly enough, working hard in the fields, tending the herds and making no trouble. Noe was pleased, and Sem was obviously delighted. And why not? Her flesh was as brown as new-turned earth, her eyes huge and black. She carried hips broader than a horse's, and legs sturdy enough to bear her all day across the parched earth. Noe gazed at her and dreamed of grandsons. From the sounds each night at the far end of the sleeping room, Sem and Bera worked hard to give those dreams flesh.

Thus it was with some anxiety that Noe watched as the seasons wheeled by, ewes were rutted and lambs weaned, and still Bera's stomach remained as flat as Sem's. Seasons became years. Sem's beard started graying, and Bera's black ringlets followed suit. Noe despaired that he had read the signs wrong.

Bera finds her voice.—I haven't seen my father since I was a child. Is that all?

—Mm? No, of course not. I may need to ask you to do something.

Bera says nothing, observant, reserved.

—Your father's lands are to the south, no?

—Very far. Many weeks' travel.

Noe strains, but can recall no lands south of Canaan.—Distant indeed, he says lamely, wishing they had discussed this before. But everyone stays off the topic: Bera's past seems likely to contain unpleasantness.

Noe gropes for words, something he is unused to. Somehow his firstborn's wife has this effect on him.—You may be asked to return there.

Bera regards him placidly.—I would prefer not to.

—You understand what I have to do.

—Build a ship.

—Yes.

—And you wish me to return to my father's lands. For animals, I imagine.

Noe spreads his hands.—Exotic creatures live in your country. Monsters I have only heard whispers of, lizards with necks as tall as a man and birds feathered in diamonds and silver. Cats that can outrun lightning. Plus gazelles and monkeys and wild dogs and so on.

—And you want all these things.

—As many as possible. Else all shall be lost.

She has her arms crossed beneath pillowy breasts, standing with legs wide, feet planted. One foot tapping. Despite her casual pose, Noe thinks she seems interested.
—It's a long journey, and a dangerous one.

—I know. Noe's shoulders sag.—I'll not be able to spare Sem, and you won't have much money.

—That makes it easy, she says, deadpan.

—Consider it, Noe says.—Think on the quickest route there, and how to get the animals. Seek your father's help.

He stands to go. She says, There is a problem.

—There are many problems.

She nods, acquiescing.—I despise my father. I would like him dead. I hope he is.

Noe stares with hard eyes like blue coals.—These are sinful things to say.

—My father traded me as a slave. He sent me away to be gang-rutted at age seven, while he collected warriors and plotted his next campaign. These are sinful things to *do*.

Noe breathes to steady himself.—We are faced with a desperate situation. The past is past.

—Undeniably, she nods.

—You must forgive, he says.

—Perhaps, she shrugs. Then smiles coldly.—Perhaps not.

Noe leaves the house quickly, shaken, wondering what he will do if the girl fails him. Rely on God, of course. He scans the sunrise horizon, checking for clouds, seeking an omen. He finds neither.

Noe provisions the mule and rides north for six days.

The sun beats him like a rod. Around him the land quivers and ripples as if still just an idea in God's mind. The hills east of his homestead disappear the first morning, others appear before him and slowly recede in his wake. Noe eats on the mule's back, sleeps hunched over its neck as it makes its way slowly on.

Noe has made this journey before but not in this hot season. He wonders if he has made a mistake, then exiles that thought. If he has made a mistake, it means that God has too.

On the third day his waterskins run dry. He licks his lips and tastes blood.

On the fourth day the mule staggers into the shade of a palm thicket, in the midst of which is sunk a silty spring of fresh water. Noe and the mule lower their heads into it together. Noe slurps, cries, prays at more or less the same time.

When he next opens his eyes, night has fallen. The mule is leaning into a palm tree, snoring gently. Flies industriously burrow in its nostrils. Clearer-headed than he has felt in days, Noe refills the waterskins and washes down a few dates. I have passed through the fire, he thinks, and am the stronger for it. I have been tested and not found wanting. I was lost, but now am found.

He sleeps again, sets out the following evening, traveling all night. The moon makes it easy to navigate. By sunrise the mountains to the north hove into view, and by midmorning he is close enough to make out a few dim structures. The desert's strange rippling perspective causes them to appear closer than they are, but Noe expects this; he understands that the buildings are enormous beyond any human scale. He rests the mule at another spring that evening, cleaner than the first, then rouses himself before dawn to ride into the foothills.

They are waiting for him. They have marked his approach, of course, and could have assisted his journey the last day or two. He does not take it amiss that they have not: it isn't their way. They do not walk with God.

There are two of them, tall as cedar trees, sprawled on a tangle of boulders. One grins down at him as Noe clambers up the hill, red-faced, staff in sweaty hand. The other glowers. Somewhere below waits the mule, grazing.

—Greetings, Grandfather, says the first with a smile.

—Good journey to you, offers the second, grudgingly.

—Peace on you both, gasps Noe. His head reaches their knees. He pauses to wipe his face with a corner of his headcloth, then rewraps it. Even at mid-morning, the sun burns like an accusation.

—What brings you here, Grandfather? grins the giant. He sports a great tangle of black curly ringlets that tumble to his shoulders. When he smiles, which is often, dimples crease his cheeks. His tunic is cleaner than his ill-tempered friend's and embroidered with a decorative floral pattern. —It is a warm season for travel.

—I come for timber, Noe says.—To build a ship. And pitch as well, though that can come later.

—Timber and pitch, nods the giant. He glances at his companion, who is leaner and, if anything, taller than the first. And bald. Noe tries to read the look that passes between them, but as he must look up at them, silhouetted against the morning sky, their faces are shadowed. —How much do you need?

—Enough for a ship three hundred cubits long, fifty wide, thirty tall.

—That's a large ship indeed, Grandfather.

—So it is.

The two giants loom over him. The bald one says, Whose cubits? Yours or mine?

Noe hasn't entirely caught his breath after his recent ascent.—I don't understand.

The bald giant stretches out an enormous arm. It hangs over Noe like a blade, heavenly or hellish, threatening to drop.—A cubit is the distance from elbow to fingertip. Whose cubits do you want, yours or mine?

—Imagine three hundred of *those*, Grandfather, says the smiling giant.—There's a mighty ship for you, all right.

Noe closes his eyes to their cackling. Things were much clearer when God was explaining. He opens his eyes and says, Mine.

—Well then, they shrug. The curly one says, That's not so much. We could collect that much timber from the mountains in, what, four days?

—Three, suggests his companion.

—Two.

—One.

—Let's do it this morning.

The dimpled giant clenches mule-sized hands between house-sized thighs and leans forward. Noe feels the man's breath wash him like a waterfall.—The two of us could have the wood you want by afternoon. The pitch will take longer to distill. How you'll get it all home is beyond me.

—Perhaps you have some oxen, Noe suggests.

—Perhaps we do. And drays for hauling. And what do you have to pay for all this?

—At the moment, nothing. But I'll send my son with some goats. You know where my farmstead is, so don't think I won't pay.

The two giants exchange incredulous glances.—Goats?

—Hors d'oeuvres, laughs the gaunt one.—Pffft.

Noe remains silent. He has nothing more to offer, so he waits for the Infinite to lend a hand.

The friendlier of the giants, the one with the curls and the dimples, addresses Noe again.—Why are you doing this, anyway? Building a ship. I thought you were a farmer.

A lesser man might be tempted to lie. A greater man might proudly refuse to answer. Noe is an ordinary man, six hundred years old, conversing with giants, touched by God. He says, The Lord intends to destroy all the earth.

—Then why do you want a boat?

—To survive.

The giants regard each other. The lean one bends forward to demand: And us?

—You will be destroyed also, and all your kin and all your works.

Perhaps his gravity impresses them. There is a pause.

—Unless of course you heed me, Noe adds helpfully.

They look away as if embarrassed by this tiny bearded hornet. Their hands tap their knees. The dimpled one, not smiling now, asks, If we are to be destroyed, then why should we help you?

For a moment Noe wonders how to answer. Then something tells him.

—So you are not forgotten forever, he says.—So that when we survive to tell our story, and our sons and grandsons do the same, your memory will live on within us.

No one speaks for a while then, while the sun rains down on everything.

4
Sem

Four years will change a man. The first time I clap eyes
on Cham I don't even recognize him. He has filled out,
thicker across the shoulders from all that heavy work. But
mainly it's the beard. Bushy thing in all directions, and
lank black hair past his shoulders. Little piece of string
tied round his forehead. He looks like a . . . I don't know
what he looks like. But he has no new freckles or warts,
which is good, and his eyes are the same sea-green as
before. Even better. So there's no need to worry on that
score.

He recognizes me immediately.—Sem! he hollers, and
wraps me up in a hug that's near to cracking my spine.—
Adam's rib, Sem, it's good to see you.
  —The beard suits you, I tell him, though it doesn't.
Makes his face look like a stork's nest, but no point saying
so.
  He pushes me back, grinning that big toothy smile.
It's funny to see it pop out from the beard, but it's good

too. Memories well up. The two of us in the sleeping room, rain slashing outside, Mother and Father humped under the blanket . . .

—So! It's not the old man is it?

—What?

His face has gone somber, big green eyes frog-popping out of his head.—He's not gotten sick has he? I always figured him to live forever.

—Oh no. Father's fine, Mother too.

—Good. Come on, I'll take you to see Ilya.

The famous Ilya. I admit I'm curious. Word came of the marriage two years back but we have none of us met her.

He leads me by the hand through the streets. This is some seaside village at the mouth of the River Za, I don't know its name. Or if it has a name. In fact I wasn't even sure this was the right village, never having been here before. But then when I was riding in from the desert I saw two larks chasing a dove, so I knew I had it right.

It's not a bad-looking place. There's a tang to the air, and the caw of endless seagulls, and a few more shades to the complexions of the people than I'm used to. But that's to be expected in a place this size.—How many people in this town, Cham? Dozens, must be.

He laughs up at me like old times.—Keep your voice down. There's hundreds in the town alone, that's not counting the sailors passing through and the merchants buying and selling.

Hundreds, he says.—Adam's rib.

He laughs again.—I thought you didn't swear.
—Not in front of Father I don't.

Away from the waterfront lies a maze of narrow lanes lined
with mud huts and a few brick structures. Some of them
are two stories tall, and I crane my neck to get a look at
them. Underfoot is pure mud. Everywhere are people and
mules, drays, laundry hanging on lines. Children dodging
through it all . . . —How do you keep from going mad
in this place?

—You get used to it, he assures me. We cut left into
an even narrower alleyway between two tall mud taverns.
—Mind the shit.

—Too late, I mutter.

Halfway up the lane, a white cat with no tail leaps
onto a windowsill. A little tremor of apprehension passes
through me at *that*, you may believe.

We stop before an open doorway.—My castle, Cham says,
and ushers me through.

It's a single room, sleeping pallet at the far wall, kitchen
things in one corner. Beneath the only window is a small
round table with stools. Bare enough but clean, the walls
limewashed and the floor sprinkled with fresh sand. Father
would approve, and I do too.—It's nice, I say, then stop.

—Ilya, he says.—My brother Sem.

I have seen her already. She sits on one of the stools,
beside the window so the light falls on her from outside.
There is no mistaking the signs.

*　*　*

At first I think she is very old. Then I realize her face is unlined, the skin taut. She regards me evenly for a moment.—Peace upon you, brother, she says.—Welcome into our home.

—Peace on you, I answer back.—Thank you for your hospitality.

—Why this formality? Cham cries, slapping my back.—Sit, sit. Some wine if we have it, love. Sem, you'll take it with honey?

—A trifle, I say, and weakened with water. I have much to tell and must keep a clear head.

—That's my brother, Cham grins. Ilya smiles back. I am miserable. My hands twist in my lap. I cannot bear to look at her and I don't know how to broach the subject with Cham. She is obviously given over to a demon, maybe dead already or walking damned. Is it possible he doesn't know?

After a time I regain my composure. The wine helps to steady my nerves, and the honey refreshes. The woman says very little. Just what you would expect.

—Have some fruit, she suggests, laying a platter of unfamiliar shapes and colors on the table. Her hands bearing the tray end in dead white fingers like grubs.—It comes from all over the world.

—Thank you, I murmur. I cannot look at her face but at least my stomach has settled.

—So what news from home? Cham demands.

I force myself to attend to the matter at hand.—Cham, you must return with me. Immediately.

—Oh really? Why?

—Because . . . You just have to is all.

I try to remember what Father said about this. There were several things. I blurt, He wants you to. In fact he's dying.

—No he's not, says Cham.

—How do *you* know? I snap.

—Because you told me, remember? He grins his square-toothed yellow smile and begins peeling one of the fruits.—I asked if anything was wrong and you told me no. You wouldn't lie to a direct question, though I don't know why you're trying now.

—Oh.

—So, he says, why don't you explain what's *really* going on?

I sigh. Cham always has been the clever one.

—Fortunately, he says after much explanation, we were planning a trip home already. We'll just go a few months sooner than expected.

—And stay a few months longer, Ilya says quietly, with a lopsided smile. Her teeth are prominent and pointed.

Cham shrugs.—If this rain actually materializes.

—Why would you doubt it? I ask them.

Once he has made up his mind, it all happens swiftly. I stay the night with them, though I admit to sleeping little enough with *her* in the room. . . . Next morning Cham goes to his job to announce his departure. The afternoon is spent buying provisions and a mule for the two of them. Cham seems set on a dun-colored mare with a cropped ear. Just how ignorant is he? And the boy selling it has a lisp, no less. Fortunately I intercede, and they settle on a sturdy gray with bloodshot eyes. Better safe than sorry, I say.

They already have a donkey to carry their bags. These are filled mainly with Cham's tools, which he shows me with a bit too much pride. They are all carved handles and metal blades and unlike anything I have seen before.

—Impressive, I say as I gingerly finger the adze, or the ax, or the awl, I forget which.

—Careful, he tells me.—That cost a year's wages.

He lashes a long heavy coil of orange metal onto the donkey's back.—We'll use this to make nails. Japheth can learn how, I'll need you to help me strip the lumber.

At home our tools are made of stone or wood. Mother's cookpot is an exception, and Father's castration knife.—Where do you find such things as this?

—There's great advantage to living in a port village, he grins. With a wink at his ghastly wife he adds, You get all kinds of unusual items floating in from overseas.

Just before sunset we leave, after the bats have taken to the air but before the evening star is visible. We make our way east on the track I'd ridden in on two days before. The sea falls behind us, its roar dying to a murmur, then to nothing.

Ilya rides behind Cham, her arms loose around his waist, her face leaning against the slope of his shoulder. I still cannot bring myself to look upon her. She says sleepily, Is your father prone to pranks such as these?

31

My stomach clenches but Cham just hoots.—Do you hear that Sem?

—I hear.

—Our father, he answers his so-called wife, has a special relationship with Yahweh, it's true. Most of the time I think the old boy likes to tell God what he's doing wrong. Every so often, God has an answer for him.

Ilya smiles.

—But he takes it awfully serious, Cham continues, and so does Sem here.

I say nothing. It has gotten dark and I concentrate on the trail and the signs.

—Isn't that right Sem?

—Right enough.

He says to Ilya, So it's best to keep any talk of pranks to yourself, love. Best to speak of *visions*, it's more respectful.

—I see, says Ilya.

—And yeah, Cham adds, he gets them from time to time. None for a while now, but I gather when he was young they came thick and fast. It's why he moved out of his father's house and took to farming that diabolical patch by the edge of the desert.

—Watch it, Cham, I say. He may be the clever one but I'll only bear so much.

The moon rises, throwing a watery cast over the trail, the scrub, the low rolling plains. We ride in silence. Cham's gray mule moves through the night like a stain of quicksilver. Cham's hair and beard leak into the dark, leaving him looking like some headless demon. And her . . .

Ilya's own head glows in the night, her nimbus throwing unholy highlights up at the stars. Like nothing so much as a challenge to God Himself.

5
Noe

And Noe did all the things which God commanded him.

GENESIS 6:22

Noe returns on his mule to the homestead, leading six teams of oxen dragging thirty cords of timber. The pitch has been promised for later. His journey back has taken twelve days, traveling at night, and has taxed both him and his beasts to the very last of their endurance. Within sight of the hills in back of his lands, his mule collapses beneath him, dead as iron. Noe tumbles heavily and does not rise. Half the oxen join him.—Lord, I have strived to do your bidding, he tries to say. But the words lodge in his throat like dust.

He wakes to dimness, the indoor mustiness of the sleeping chamber. In the next room, murmuring voices. Nearby, a frantic rustling: he cranes his neck to see his youngest, Japheth, rutting his wife Mirn. Noe croaks something and Japheth, his face a rictus of effort, gasps, Yahweh! before collapsing beside the girl.

Mirn straightens up, adjusting her shift round her ankles.—Japheth, he's *awake.*

—Mmm?

Noe croaks again. Mirn, round-faced and olive-complected, smiles shyly and tucks a strand behind her ear.—I'll get the others, she says, and scurries off, bare feet padding against the earthen floor.

—Japheth, Noe manages.

—Mmm?

—Japheth!

The boy's eyes open and he raises himself on his elbows.—Oh, hello Da.

Noe's voice is fast returning.—There's work to do. There'll be time enough to know your wife later, right now we've got to work together. Do you understand?

—Sure Da, the child grins.—Anything you say.

The family crowds through the door, surrounding him, filling the dim sleeping room with their concern. Sem and Bera, Japheth and Mirn. Noe's own wife, pressing a cup of water toward him, and Cham, whom he hasn't seen these four years past. And this, this apparition. This specter.

—Cham, he manages, and sips the water. His throat loosens.

Cham inclines his head.—Abba. My wife. Ilya, my father.

Noe drinks the water and considers the girl. Tall, for one thing, taller than any of them. A willow. And color-less. Her flesh is chalk-pale, fishlike, so that a delicate tracery of red and blue is visible beneath it, like the veins of a leaf. Hair straight down her back like a wash of silver, like a spring sweeping past a block of quartz. Eyes of the palest gray, lashes all but invisible. Only her lips are kissed with a brush of pink. Noe notices that Sem is keeping his distance, watching her, then in turn watching Noe's reaction to her. Well. That was Sem for you.

Noe says, Peace on you, daughter.

—And you, she nods.—Thank you.

—You are from one of the northern tribes, I believe?

—Far to the north, she agrees.—Where snow is as common as sand is here.

He decides not to ask what snow is. Some kind of plant most likely.—And my son has made himself husband to you?

—So he has, Abba.

—And is he a good husband?

She smiles easily, revealing delicate incisors and canines as pointed as any fox's.—I have no complaints.

—Good. Noe smiles too, and the room's somber mood lifts a little. Only Sem still looks uneasy.—If you've any reason to change your mind, seek me out.

—I'll remember that.

Cham clears his throat.—When you get the chance, Abba, maybe you can reassure Sem here that she's not a demon from Hell come to suck dry our immortal souls.

Japheth guffaws. Sem blushes, while Noe's wife clucks her tongue.—I never said—Sem begins.

—You should've heard him, Cham continues restlessly. —Going on about, Brother, do you know what she is? Do you know who hast begot her? I tell him, sure I do: her father, a trader from the north who died in a shipwreck off the Kittim, that's who.

Japheth hides his head in Mirn's stomach, giggling helplessly.

—In my own defense, Sem begins ponderously, all the signs were there. And you must admit, Father, she's unlike any we've ever seen in these lands.

—But that's why I like her, Cham says. With a wink at Ilya, who winks back.

Noe holds up his hands.—Enough. Ilya, forgive my superstitious son. He means no harm.

She inclines her head with a soft smile.—None taken.

Noe pushes on.—Now we're all here, we've plenty of work to do. A ship to build, and animals to gather. I propose we divide up the labor and get started.

—You're not well, his wife chides, putting a hand to his forehead.

He waves her away.—Time to rest later. We've a stack of materials outside and we know what we're to do with them. Expeditions must be sent to gather the Lord's creatures. Nothing's to be gained through delaying. This is one storm we don't want to be caught out in, hm?

No one argues.

6
Bera

*Of all clean beasts take seven and seven, the
male and the female.*

GENESIS 7:2

—God will provide, my husband's father says.—Now go.

And that's that. He leaves me to travel some twelve
hundred miles on a handful of copper weights, a few
weeks' dried provisions and a donkey as company. I'm
expected to return with no less than breeding families of
every beast in creation. The problem with people who
think that God will provide, is that they think God will
provide.

I ride south, keeping to the established trade routes,
making for the finger of water that pokes north from the
southern sea. Wrapped tight in a white pilgrim's cloak, I
hunker on my donkey. (Not even a mule.—They're needed
for the heavy work, he tells me before I leave, and of
course has no answer when I ask, What exactly do you
call this?)

The landscape shifts as I pass. In the north everything's bleached, as if proximity to God has drained it of
color. Even the sky is white, and the clothes people wear

are tan and gray, the natural tints of linen and wool. But in the south the natives dye their cloth with mustard and indigo till the people quite resemble the flycatchers and rollers that sweep along the sky in babbling clusters.

After ten days I have covered perhaps two hundred miles. The semi-desert is behind me, and I ride through a grassland of pale green streaked with yellow. Butterflies loop drunkenly around me, orange, aquamarine, blue-black. All seem to be making better progress than I am. (My donkey is willing but he is, after all, a donkey.) And some days after this I reach the sea.

At a tumbledown fishing village I bargain for passage on a cargo barge. The captain is a taciturn old specimen, withered and black and prone to predictions of doom. He is naked but for a wrap around his loins, and he limps.
—I have little to offer in payment, I say.

He shrugs.—There's room enough aboard, and besides, Bokataro will look upon me with benevolence if I perform a kindness.

Bokataro, I gather, is the local idol.
—On the other hand, he yawns, y'never know. Bokataro is unpredictable in her moods. She could anger at my helping an infidel, and all could end in catastrophe.

The captain's name is Ulm. I request that he alter his route and take me south, but he refuses. His plan is to sail out the mouth of this little gulf, then run across open sea to the eastern shore. In all, perhaps a hundred miles. Ulm is adamant that his barge is incapable of more.

Perhaps he is right. Though squat and sturdy, the

vessel is barely thirty cubits long, and squeaks alarmingly as it bobs on the tide. Bales covered with blue tarpaulins are lashed to the deck, leaving little room for the five or six sailors to maneuver the lines of the sails. There are two of these, a big, triangular canvas in the center of the deck, and a smaller one up front.

The plan is to provision the ship tonight and leave at dawn, but I wake to a night filled with frantic shouts and heaving swells that threaten to swamp the vessel where we're moored. With a jerk the landing lines snap, and the boat shudders away from shore into howling blackness. Hazy clouds gauze the moon's silver sliver, leaving just enough light to see that there's not nearly enough light to see. (Bad omen that, my husband would say.)

The sails had been left unfurled, and now crewmen heave back on their lines to keep them angled and, I suppose, to prevent the masts snapping like kindling. Ulm is at the rear with his other two men, big ones both of them, hunched over the tiller. This beam is eight cubits long, attached to a big paddle used to steer, or in this case used to prevent the boat from flipping belly up. The beam thrashes in their arms like a criminal.

I catch hold of Ulm's shoulder and holler above the wind, What can I do?

A house-sized swell crashes over the gunwale, sending us all to our knees. Somehow nobody is flung into the maelstrom. Ulm's dour screech rasps in my ear: Y'can get your infidel cunt off my vessel, y'damn harpy!

He certainly sounds like he means it. I flounder my

way back amidships and find a spot to wedge into, between a pair of tightly bound bales. Grasping the lines that anchor them to the deck, I burrow forward with my feet and back with my shoulders. The bales contain wool or cloth, and cup me like a pair of well-meaning hands.

After a time the clouds recede and the stars burn fiercely. The sea-swell settles, so the glittering water throws back ten thousand firefly-gleams of starlight, a pattern of white sparks in the blue-black that would be quite lovely if we weren't fighting to stay alive. It's only after some time that I realize we're not, in fact, fighting to stay alive. The barge runs quite smoothly now, with barely a shudder of its decks. The wind is supernaturally steady, and we are no longer drenched by bombardments of water.

Oddly, the sky pales to our left, though sunrise should be astern as we bear westward. Has the captain changed his plans? Still the wind presses us on. Plumes of white ripple past the bow like egret feathers. I've never seen anything (charging horse, waterfall, avalanche) move faster. We have kept this pace half the night at least. Over my left shoulder, pale turquoise and grapefruit colors spill into the air.

I stand. Everything is aching and stiff, but everything works. The sailors still man the boom lines, murmuring softly among themselves. Ulm alone hangs on the tiller, staring ahead, then glaring at me directly.—Come here, witch, he shouts.

With some misgivings I approach. He watches me the way some men look on sin: with equal measures of revulsion and keen interest.—What manner of demon are you?

There seems no good answer to this.

—Well, y'wanted to go south, he spits, chin jutting petulantly at the water ahead.—And so we are.

—Turn west if you wish, I tell him.—I can find a caravan from there.

He snorts.—We'd be feeding the fish by midday, witch. As y'well know yourself.

From this I gather that the vessel would be torn apart if he did anything but let the wind push it.

—Only thing keeping me from putting you over the side this instant, he says, is not knowing what y'could do if y'had reason to be angry with me.

I consider a moment.—Best for you not to find out, I say.

I leave him uttering prayers (or curses?) to Bokataro, and return to my nest among the bales. The sun is well up, the sea a white-streaked bruise beneath a pale sky. The sailors' hunched shoulders and broad black backs are set resolutely against me. A strange feeling it is too, to earn the fear of large men. I imagine I'll get used to it. God knows how often it's been the other way around.

No one speaks to me that day. The sailors take spells on the lines and eye the canvas warily. I eat a few dates and some dried meat, glad I've brought my own food.

Sunset is oozing red like a scab when the captain next addresses me. He stands silhouetted against the sun's failing glow, favoring his bad knee.—Reckon we've gone a hundred miles.

—That's a lot?

His voice is a mix of wonder and fear.—As much as any vessel could reasonably expect to travel in five days. There's not been a squall or crosswind since last night, just a steady blow from the north. Never seen the like.

He spits.—Don't ask me what's keeping us together either, because I don't know.

I think of Sem's God, and Noe's, and say: I do.

—Yeah. I just bet y'do, he says, and limps off.

We go on like this for seven days.

At the end of it, we make landfall hundreds of leagues south of our destination. The sailors are well out of familiar territory. They're torn between despising me for having brought them to this pass, and being curious, despite themselves, about where we've gotten to. When the wind dies, we wash up along a stretch of golden sand fringed with dense leafy trees. Hills rear up distantly, blanketed with moss-green jungle. Further still, mountains faintly violet. And right along the edge of the waterline, a string of warriors like a line of onyx idols, bone necklaces cold as death, throwing arms raised, spear tips glittering wetly. Some poison or other.

—Bokataro save us all, murmurs the captain.

We drift toward shore as if pushed. Ulm seems to have given up on the idea of navigation. To me he says, Your people?

Not exactly. They're reed thin, naked as magpies, with loop earrings and heron feathers wreathing their heads. Bodies glisten black where they're not smeared with red clay or yellow stain. I recognize the warrior marks of the southern tribes. Not quite my father's people, but close. Rivals sometimes, allies at others.

Before I can think what to do next, their leader splashes ankle-deep into the water. (I know he's the leader because of the heavy ivory bracelets he wears.) In a loud clear voice he screeches: Akki akki akki!

The echoes die away. We are perhaps ten cubits from shore. With the right breeze we could drift out of range, but we don't have the right breeze. If we tried to paddle, the spears would mow us like flax.

—Akki takki nigatti! cries the warrior.

And then there is a moment as when the sun slips from behind clouds. Perhaps thirty years have passed since I spoke my father's tongue, yet suddenly the words fill my head.

In their language I say as best I can: My name is Bera. This gets their attention.—I seek my father, I tell them.

The warrior leader squints.—And who is he?

—Pra. Headman of the lands where the rivers join.

There is a stirring among the warriors, glances exchanged. Some spears are lowered.

—We know him, the man replies.—He is allied to our headman by marriage. Why should we believe you are kin to Pra?

—Take me to him. He'll recognize me.

Or so I hope, but only a fool would say that.

—Soon Pra will join his ancestors, the warrior says.

Meaning he is ill. I feel no sadness, but it will complicate matters if he dies quickly.—All the more reason for me to see him. I have journeyed a great distance, and will not be denied.

The warrior has a gap between his teeth that shows when he wrinkles his nose, which he does now.—There is rivalry for Pra's lands and wealth, he says.—Perhaps you are coming to add more dissent among his sons and their wives.

—I have no interest in lands or wealth, I say. With a gesture to the baffled sailors behind me I add, Do they look like an army?

Amid general laughter, the warrior demands, Then what is it you want, Bera daughter of Pra?

Not knowing what else to say, I tell them the truth.

I barely knew him when he traded me like livestock. I was the third daughter of the twentieth wife of a man who valued only sons to fight his wars. So when I am led to this man's bedside in the royal hut, I am quite unmoved. He is an old animal reduced to component parts: white hair and yellow eyes, gray flesh, brown teeth. I have slaughtered goats that meant more to me than this.

The old woman who attends him shakes my elbow impatiently and I say, Father, it is I. Your daughter Bera who you sent away long ago. Do you remember?

The yellow eyes are cloudy and unfocused.—Mmmhmm?

—Father, I repeat (though it nearly chokes me to call him this).—Father, I seek your blessing. I need permission to gather animals from your lands. Not to kill them, just to collect.

45

—Ehh? His eyes widen at this.—The osso? You wish to hunt the osso?

—Everything, Father, for a great menagerie being built far away in the desert.

This stumps him. (In fact it rather stumps me too, when I think about it too closely). He falls silent so long, I wonder if he's forgotten me. But suddenly he says, Bera. Daughter of Gret?

I have no idea. My mother died young and I never heard her name. Who was this Gret, I wonder. A favored wife whose passing he has long mourned? Or a shrewish traitor who deserved her execution? (Buried to her neck beside a nest of fire ants, perhaps. Dollops of honey crowning her head.) I haven't an inkling.

But I must say something. So I take a chance and say, Yes.

He falls silent again. A fly strolls across his gray-brown forehead, as if he is made of dung.—The menagerie, is it?

—Yes, I say carefully, but I'm not sure I've heard right.

His fingers flutter.—So be it. I have no need of it now. Take the menagerie to the desert. Anything she wants, it is hers.

The old woman bows.—Sire.

Outside I say to her, I don't understand what just happened.

The woman is shriveled like a fig but her black eyes are merry.—Oh I think you do.

—I only wish to collect animals, I begin.

—That's been done for you, she interrupts.—All you need do is take them away.

I feel quite baffled.—I think you'd better show me.

The menagerie is laid out in circles one inside the next, with the fiercest beasts in the middle. They are kept in cages of bamboo, and they all look like monsters to me.

There are huge cats, dun-yellow or spotted or plain black, who snarl hideously at our approach. Then cages with enormous monkeys, frightful beasts with black fur and soulful eyes, then the enormous, ivory-bearing beasts called osso by my father, and nightmarish water-dwelling lizards fifteen cubits long. Lethargic, they are. Then massive-jawed water pigs. Flightless birds taller than Sem. Gazelles twenty cubits tall, with necks as long as a man. And this is only the innermost circle.

The old woman guides me through, telling me the names.—Osso. Dorn. Pelnar, kara, eft. Do you know none of the names of these animals you want so badly?

—Apparently not, I tell her. I try to remember my father-in-law's story of his ancestors. Adam and his wife went forth and gave names to them, or unto them, but I do not recall hearing of anything called pelnar or osso or dorn.

All manner of little gazelles fill the other cages, and wild scavenger dogs and strange-bodied, hard-shelled creatures with naked rats' tails. Tortoises and squirrels. Wild oxen and oversized, clumsy gray abominations with horns on their noses. The kind of thing a child might draw if you said, Make me a picture of something ridiculous.

I am quite speechless. The old woman stands beside me, cackling at my reaction.—He gifted it all to you, she says gleefully.—Hope you have someplace to put it.

That afternoon I return to Ulm's barge. The captain has filled his time by haggling with locals willing to trade stacks of ivory for a few waterlogged bales of wool.
—Come with me, I tell him.

—I'm in the middle of negotiations.

—Don't make me angry, I warn.

When he sees the menagerie he says, Now what?

—Now we take it back.

He laughs.—Not on *my* vessel you won't.

I say, We will build rafts.

—Rafts.

—Float them in a line, like a desert caravan.

—Caravan, he says. He stands there chewing his tongue, as if wondering what Bokataro would have to say about all this.

I say, The sooner we start, the sooner we're done.

It takes us four days to manhandle those cages, hundreds of them, through meandering jungle trails to the shore. Trees are felled, tall and thick-boled, and tough, stringy vines woven into ropes to bind them. Gangs of natives stack the trees into double-thick squares forty cubits on a side. They don't look terribly seaworthy, but they float.

—Loaded properly they'll be steady enough, Ulm assures me. (It's easy to see why he's a captain: he adores giving orders.)—Barring storms of course. The trick is to balance the weight. . . . And away he goes, hollering commands.

At length four rafts are ready and the animals loaded. Half of one raft is set aside for supplies (forage for the plant-eaters and a couple dozen apprehensive goats for the predators). The whole thing looks as unlikely a sight as I ever expect to see.

—Nothing's sinking, I say to Ulm.

—Yet, he grumbles cheerfully.

Somehow I'm not surprised when the breeze starts from the south. Gentle at first, barely ruffling the hair on my legs, then stronger, as if urging us to leave.

Before we go the old woman appears at my side bearing two tiny black bundles.—Take these as well, she says.—The mother died in childbirth, and their father hates them in consequence.

—I can't possibly, I tell her.—What would I do with them?

—Raise them, she cackles, as if it's all quite funny.

Somehow they are in my arms, a boy and a girl, shriveled and black as bats.—But how will I feed them?

She nudges my teat.—This is decoration?

—We'd best go, Ulm calls. Water is rippling where the wind catches it. On the rafts, the animals mutter.

I find a spot among the stacked ivory on Ulm's deck and settle in. The sailors watch me carefully but are more cheerful than before. They know how much they stand to profit.

I still hold these droopy children in my arms, watching me with half-open mouths and half-closed eyes. I set them on my lap and, on impulse, hike my tunic to my neck. The children wave their little starfish hands and twist their heads as if they have seen the promised land. I lift them again and their mouths clamp on my nipples, which sprout and harden beneath their slurping tongues.

—Sorry, little ones, I tell them.—Nothing there. We'll find some goat's milk for you, if you can abide it.

But then I stop talking, because something shudders through my breast. A little ripple, a pleasant throbbing. Pain also, a little rip of something wet. When I look down, the boy has pulled his head back from my teat. Watery white drops trickle down his chin. More dribbles from my nipple.

For a long time everything seems to stop moving. There is a tightness in my midriff but the boat and the ocean have gone. There is only my teat, that toothless mouth, those blue-white drops. The corners of my eyes prickle: I feel ready to shriek in horror or laugh crazily or explode into tears. Or all three. Maybe I should pray. Maybe this would be a good time to do that.

A shadowy presence beside me. Ulm stands at the rail of the ship, carrying a carved statuette in his hand. —I have witnessed a miracle, he declares.

I mumble, So have I.

He ignores me.—More than one in fact. First that wind taking us down here, now this wind bringing us back. This isn't Bokataro's doing I'm sure.

—You're right.

With my fingertips I squeeze my own teat; a droplet traces a ghostly path down my thumb. I stare as though seeing someone else's body. Maybe I am.

Ulm says, What do you call your god, anyway?

—Just God, I say.—Or sometimes Yahweh.

He grunts.—See this? This is Bokataro.

I look up. The statuette is carved from dark wood, with animal fangs inlaid in her ferocious mouth, and six dugs spilling from her belly. In one hand she carries a spear, in the other a drinking gourd.—That's Bokataro?

Without a word he heaves the statue over the side of the boat.—That *was* Bokataro.

I wonder how I should feel about this. A little sad, certainly, as if something has been lost. But it was only a statue.

—Now, says Ulm, tell me how to go about worshiping this God of yours.

—Just talk to Him, I say.—It's what He seems to enjoy.

—And does He answer?

I almost start crying at that. The little boy has gone back to my nipple, a little stab of pain and sweetness wrapped up together. I breathe deep and force a steadiness into my voice that I don't feel.—He is fond of riddles and double meanings, and things are seldom clear.

—Figures, Ulm grunts.—What do you say to Him?

—Just let Him know you haven't forgotten Him, and tell Him thanks. He loves to hear you say thanks. He hates it when people forget that, I think, more than anything else.

—No sacrifices? Animals, prisoners, virgins?

—Nothing like that, no.

—Nor tributes? Gold left on mountaintops, anything?

I shake my head.

Ulm stares out at the water. The shore has disappeared and we're alone on the sea, empty blue-green leagues in all directions. With the rafts tied on we're moving slower than before, though smoothly enough. Probably we'll be two weeks on the return journey, and absently I hope our supplies last. (Then I remind myself, Of course they will.)

Ulm says, I'd very much like to meet this Yahweh of yours. Of ours.

—You will, I tell him.

7
Noe

Each morning Noe wakes with gummy teeth and bad breath. He sits up on his sleeping mat, runs a hand through his beard to shake out the insects, and recites this prayer.
—Thank you Lord for another day, the health to enjoy it, a labor to fill it, and a home to return to at the end of it.

Then he rises from the mat, rinses his face at the trough outside, eats his breakfast and goes round in back of the house where there used to be a mustard patch, now wilting beneath thirty cords of stacked lumber.

And every morning Japheth mutters into Mirn's ear: Thank you Lord for another day, a wet hole to enjoy, my stiff loins to fill it with, and a home to do it in. Though a field would be just as good.

—Hush, Mirn whispers.—He'll hear.

—Rut him.

Outside, Noe uses a piece of charcoal and a flat scrap of wood to sketch out a diagram: a long narrow rectangle.
—Nothing fancy. Three hundred cubits by fifty, and thirty tall.

—It's too skinny, Abba, Cham protests with a frown.
—That's a six-to-one ratio, it'll spin like a log.

Noe sighs, long and expressively.

—Hundred fifty, you'll be all right, says Cham.—Or double the diameter, but that'll need more wood.

Noe fights impatience.—The proportions are not open to discussion.

—Father, listen to Cham, urges Sem.—It's why we brought him here.

—We brought him here because I was told to construct a ship, growls Noe.—Not so that my children could argue with their father.

The sons know that tone of voice. Noe fiddles with the charcoal, drawing unnecessary lines, smudging those already there. After a time Cham mutters, As long as the swells aren't too rough, it might do. At least let me give it a flat bottom.

—As you wish, says Noe quickly.—It will be loaded belowdecks, so a flat bottom is more practical.

He draws two horizontal lines the length of the hull.—So, three compartments underneath, you see? Plus the upper deck. With a pair of doors amidships to load the animals.

—Why so big? asks Sem.

—Some of the . . . cargo will be quite large.

Noe sees the confusion flicker across Sem's face, and feels annoyance twitch across his own. To Cham he says, Forget aesthetics.

Cham chuckles.—Believe me, they're long forgotten.

—It's not a work of art, it just has to float. And it must be durable.

—Obviously, Abba.

Noe's hands flutter like moths.—The storm may be violent, and the cargo, the weight of the animals will be, ah, substantial.

Cham tugs at his flyaway beard, taking in the diagram.—It's not a proper ship at all, is it? It's a God damn barnyard in a box.

—Don't blaspheme, says Noe.

Cham shrugs.—You've any objection to a square-cut bow? More storage space that way, and more stability. Speak up now or remain forever silent.

—That's fine, says Noe.

—And no point building a cabin up on deck. It'd be more comfortable for us it's true, but it'll just make the whole thing taller and even more prone to roll. The family can stay belowdecks.

—With the animals? frowns Sem.

—Sure.

—That doesn't seem right, declares Sem.—We are different from the lesser creatures.

Cham ignores him and goes on, I'll put a little cabin near the access ladder, give it some windows. Lay in a hearth for Amma to cook on.

—Yes, fine, says Noe.

—Though God help us if we capsize, murmurs Cham.

—He will, nods Sem.

Cham rolls his eyes.—I take it you have no propulsion in mind? Navigation is out too. So no sails or tiller? Obviously oars are useless, unless you plan to have the monkeys row.

Noe considers. God said nothing about sails or oars. —I think not. We'll let the currents take us where they will.

—All right. Cham rubs his hands.—We'll start with ribs and cross braces, then the internal decks, then put the hull on. Pitching it comes last. You'll want compartments too, right? Stables and dividers and so on? So the animals don't all eat each other.

Noe nods vaguely.—Fine idea.

Cham rolls his eyes again.—We'll need a lot more wood.

—I'll work on it.

Noe walks back toward the house, satisfied but troubled too. Cham has always had a sullen streak. And where is Japheth? Time to rouse that rascal and put him to work.

Behind him he hears Sem say something like: It's not that bad, Cham, as long as it does the job.

And Cham answers: A barnyard, brother. A floating barnyard is what it is.

8
Cham

Floating coffin more like. Has there ever been a vessel such as this? Forget aesthetics, he tells me. What a joke.
   —Give us a hand with this timber, Sem, and throw the ax here while you're at it. And where the hell is Japheth?

9
Noe

Noe scans for clouds, sees none. It has become such a habit that his neck now aches without relent.

He squats against the wall of the eating room with the wife. He appears outwardly calm but inside he is counting problems. There are many. He wonders if the wife is fooled by his false serenity. Probably not. One thing Noe will say for his wife: she isn't fooled by much.

Noe's mental list of problems looks like this. 1. Need wood. 2. Need pitch. The giants were supposed to bring it, but no sign of them has been seen so far. 3. Need supplies for the family. 4. Need supplies for the animals. 5. Need animals, and no sign of them either, nor the girls sent to gather them. 6. Japheth acting the fool. 7. Cham acting tight-lipped and grumpy. 8. Sem lacking imagination. 9. Ilya as flat-bellied as Bera. Or himself for that matter. Noe has trouble seeing the point in God's saving them from destruction, if they all turn out as barren as mules. He wonders if this thought is blasphemous, decides it probably is and utters a quick prayer of apology.

It doesn't help Cham's mood that Ilya has been sent north to collect animals. Cham should understand the need, but it is his nature to act put-upon. He could take a lesson from Sem in that regard. Bera has been gone three weeks already, and Sem has simply put his head down and bulled through.

Noe sighs. The wife observes. He says, We'll need provisions.

She nods.—Those oxen are going to waste.

—Japheth and I will slaughter them tomorrow. You and Mirn dry the flesh for jerky.

—We'll need salt for that.

Another need. This makes what, ten, eleven? Noe shifts his bony rear end.—We'll find some somewhere.

—Best not to slaughter the animals beforehand.

—You think I don't know that? he snaps.

The next day a vision materializes, Dinar the peddler arriving from the far horizon, his figure wavering in the heat like an unnatural creature before finally resolving into flesh and bone and gritty sand-washed robes and sun-scarred visage. Hooded black eyes that miss nothing. Cheekbones that could cut butter.—Hear you've got a project going.

—So I do, says Noe, with a nod to the timber. A twin double-file of lonely beams stands upright in the midday glare, stretching for hundreds of cubits like a procession of doomed souls.

Dinar's horse falls upon the water trough as if dying. Dinar splashes water on his face, rinses the grit from ears and nostrils. Droplets jewel his beard. Noe thinks he looks weary.—How's business?

—Bad, says the peddler.—How's shipbuilding?

—Come in out of the sun, says Noe.—Eat with us.

After the meal Dinar says, I have little to trade. Just salt, and some seed grain which I doubt you'll need with the harvest coming on. Plus some nice sandals.

—Forget the shoes. We'll take all the other, says Noe.

Dinar lifts an eyebrow.

—Laying in supplies, Noe explains.—Poor harvest, long winter. Also, he adds, the world is to be destroyed by inundation, so we need all we can get, for later.

Dinar nods, as if this is not the first prophecy he has ever heard.—I'll give you a good price. No one's buying.

The business is concluded swiftly, bags of grain and salt stacked in the storeroom. Noe counts out a few copper pieces.—You come across any pitch or building timbers, remember me.

—Not likely, says Dinar.—I'm switching to luxury goods. Fatter margins on silk and spices and bangles and wine.

—And fatter bandits waiting to cut your throat for them, reminds Noe.

Dinar spits and says, The world's gone to Hell.

When he is gone, Noe permits himself to feel a little lighter. He is one step closer to being ready. He scans the empty sky, ignoring the pain in his neck.—Tomorrow we will butcher the oxen, he says to the wife.—You and Mirn can salt it and dry it.

It does not occur to him that the wife has planned this already.

10

Ilya

But of the beasts that are unclean two and two, male and female.

GENESIS 7:3

Men are so amusing. Show them a pack of wolves, dominated by the males, and they will say, See? It is natural for men to rule.

Fine. But produce a beehive, controlled by the queen, with males used for menial labor, and they protest, Human beings are not insects.

Yes, well.

Show them a she-cat nursing her kittens, and they say: Ah ha! Women are meant to care for the children. But remind them that that same cat ruts fifty different males in a three-day heat, and they will answer, Would you have us live like animals?

The Phoenician merchant captain who takes me north across the sea is a chubby fellow and harmless enough, and for the sake of conversation I discuss cosmology with him. His is not the God of my husband Cham, but could be His brother: old man, lightning bolts, divine retribution and so on.

—Why are you so certain your god is male? I ask him.—You've not seen him.

—Stands to reason, he says with a grin. This captain says everything with a grin. Also a tilt of the head and an open palm extended toward the listener, as though all is offered as either a concession or a gift.—Men have the power of creation in *this* world, after all.

I try not to choke.—Excuse me?

—It's the man whose seed bears fruit, he says with a grin and a tilt.

—And without the woman, I remind him, that seed is so much sap on the ground.

—And without the man, he smiles, the woman is an empty vessel waiting to be filled.

—It seems likely then, that the Creator contains elements of both. A hermaphrodite, perhaps.

This visibly perturbs him. As our discussion has no verifiable conclusion, I let the subject drop. Despite his views, the captain is a knowledgeable man, learned in various schools of astronomy and natural history, fields in which I share an interest. At one point, when I make an observation about sailing so long one might drop off the edge of the world, he smilingly extends his hand and says, That cannot happen.

—And why not?

His smile grows. He wears a robe dyed with beet-root, which emphasizes his wind-chapped cheeks.—Have you ever looked at the moon?

My journey is long, so I play his game.—I have.

—And what shape is it?

—Changeable, though generally round.

—And have you ever chanced to see the sun?

—Yes. Also circular, I add, before he can ask.

He nods.—Logic suggests what, therefore?

—Your logic is flawed, I tell him.—You forget that the sun and the moon are up there, and the earth is down here.

—Down where?

This brings me up short.—Here.

—And where is here?

Naturally I have no answer. No one does.

—Let me show you something, he says.

In the galley belowdecks he places three lemons on the table.—This is the sun, he says, and this is the earth. The earth travels around the sun, spinning as it goes.

—That's absurd.

—It gets better, he grins. He picks up the third lemon.—Here's the moon. It's a little hard to show with just two hands, but even as the earth travels around the sun, the moon travels around the earth.

Yes, well.—I liked you better when you were telling me God has testicles. What evidence have you for this?

He chuckles.—My evidence is that the sun rises and sets. That happens because the earth twirls like a top.

—And we do not feel this mighty twirling?

He shrugs.

I say, Fine. I suppose the moon rises and sets because it spins around *us* as we twirl round the sun.

—Exactly.

—Here's a simpler solution. The earth stays in one place. The sun and moon revolve around it. The earth is flat, as anybody can observe with her own eyes. Prove me wrong.

He shrugs expressively.—I can't. But I like my theory. There is a pleasant symmetry to it, like a dance, and I like the idea of all creation dancing.

So now he's a poet as well.

—It explains another thing too, he goes on.

—Which is?

He arranges the lemons in a line.—Sometimes it so happens that the moon passes between the earth and the sun. Because they're the same size, the sun disappears for a time and darkness blankets the earth. Have you never seen this?

—So I have. My brother-in-law Sem would call it a dire omen. A cause of great consternation it is, even in my homeland.

—And everywhere else. But perfectly explicable, as you can see.

He unties a tiny leatherbound scroll, covered with minute figures in a meticulous hand, column after column of them.—By my calculations, another is set to happen in exactly two weeks. At midday precisely, he declares, looking up at me with a satisfied little smile tucked between his beetroot cheeks. Like a child who has just solved a difficult sum. With relish he says: The whole world will go black.

—I shall remember that, I say with a smile. But inwardly I shudder.

—Do, he says.—And remember who told you about it, and then reconsider my dance of the heavens.

*　　*　　*

Ten days later I've landed on the north coast and fallen
in with a band of northern barbarians returning home
from a raid on one of the southern cities. They recognize me as a kindred northerner and I pass myself off as
a priestess of Oda, so they give me my own horse and
keep their hands off me. We ride at night, steering wide
of settled areas except to steal livestock. My companions
are a dozen wolf pelt–clad ruffians not at all averse to
slicing the throats of any who oppose them. I avoid the
bloodshed as best I can, but my pretense is not made any
easier by the fact that Oda, whom I represent, has a
penchant for drinking the blood of her enemies, who are
many.

My plan, such as it is, involves returning to the north-
lands and requesting the matriarchs there to provide me
with such creatures as can be found, and then returning
south with them. It's not a terribly sophisticated plan, I
admit, but it's the best I can do given the circumstances.

My escort are short on social graces and much else
besides, but their ways are familiar to me and they'll be
good protection for the journey. For two days there is
little incident, but on the third night we encounter an
isolated farmstead which offers stiffer resistance than
anticipated—the men of the household cut down three
of our number with lances, and follow on with stone axes
and stubby swords of bronze. In the moonlight the battle
is brief and bloody, but the farmers are outnumbered and
our men hack them cold without further casualties. The
women are swiftly dispatched as well. Only the children
are left, four girls and two boys, the girls barely old

enough to have begun their courses. The boys look four or five.

The men of course rape them all. I hang back, muttering curses in Cham's tongue which I hope these pigs take as imprecations to Oda.

The children are, mercifully, stupefied when the men are finished. The warriors fire the thatch roofs, and a couple draw their swords to slice the children's throats when the commander orders, Wait.

Thank God, I think.

—Our priestess should do it, the commander says. —It is Oda's will, after all.

They face me. The commander has ropes of sandy hair trailing to his shoulders like vipers, and bits of leather sheathing arms and breast. A little nub remains where his nose has been sliced off.—Well, priestess?

I breathe deep.—Oda commands against this.

The men shift their feet. The commander's eyes flicker in the firelight.—Interesting. The last priestess we knew, the one who died bravely at our side in battle, told us just the opposite.

The men murmur and nod.

—She told us to kill Oda's enemies at every opportunity. But then she also fought with us, and didn't hide behind her horse at the first sign of danger. She was a true priestess.

—As am I.

The commander sneers. Brown stubs line his mouth. The holes in his face, where his nose used to be, gape obscenely.—I don't think so.

Warriors cluster around. In desperation I fight to keep

my voice steady and say, Think carefully on what you do. Oda will be displeased if you abuse her servant.

Grinning, they pin my arms, then bind my wrists and throw me over one of the horses.—We'll see, says the commander.

We ride through the night. I'm nauseated and heaving when they push me to the ground at daybreak, my stomach long since emptied, bruised from the battering of the animal's haunches. The men gather around again, fingering their loins.

—Listen to me, I say, don't do this. Save yourselves. They laugh.

I have had all night to plan what to say.—The sun disappears today. Touch me now, and it goes forever.

—Balls, says one of the men, opening my legs. But his fellows hold him back.

—What's this? the commander demands. He cocks his head as if sniffing the wind with his absent nose.—What about the sun?

I pray to Yahweh that the Phoenician captain had his figures right.—At midday, Oda swallows the sun. Set me free, and I will beseech her to bring it back. Touch me now, or kill me, and it departs forever.

The men glance among themselves. They are a superstitious lot: even talking about this has gotten them nervous. Some of them flick their fingers in the gesture meant to ward off evil.

—Balls, says the man who was ready to take me before, but it sounds like a question.

—All right, says the commander abruptly. Perhaps he

senses that he needs to fortify the morale of his men.
—We wait till midday then. If you're right, we'll throw
ourselves on the mercy of Oda. If you're lying, well.

He cups his testicles with a hairy hand.—All the more
time to prepare our weapons, right men?

They all laugh. Too loud.

And so it is tremendously satisfying to see this crew of
motherless cretins drop to the earth when the sun does,
in fact, begin to slither out of sight. Like a snake down
its hole, I think. Some of them tremble violently, or sob
like children choking on their own fear. One of them shits
his wolfskin. Fine. I must remember to never, ever say
anything bad about Phoenicians.

We're in a little clearing on a hillside, with a good
view of the valley opening up green and lurid below. Now
a shadow rolls down the far hillside toward that valley,
ponderous, like Death itself. The warriors point, gag, cry.

The sun is two-thirds gone, eaten away as by some
huge invisible monster, when the noseless commander
throws himself at my feet.—Before Oda I prostrate myself.

Yes, well.—What good do you think that will do? You
have insulted her priestess.

His face when he raises it to me is wet, his eyes
crazed.—I'll do anything. Don't take it away.

I remain placid. The sun grows still more emaciated,
the sky twilight-gloomy. Shadow reaches the valley floor
and creeps toward us.—I will ask Oda her desire.

So I stand for a time, back stiff and eyes closed, arms
crossed overhead as I've seen the priestesses do. Behind

my eyelids I hear the rustle of the men as they shift to gaze at the sky, then the valley below us. The air is eerily still. All at once there is a chorus of quiet moans. I open my eyes. It is night. Stars glimmer. The sun is gone.

—This is what you will do, I announce in a clear voice.—Accompany me to my destination. There I have a great labor to perform, if the matriarchs allow it. You will not question what I do or why. You will assist me.

—Anything, the commander says.

—You will harm no one without cause. We will take food when necessary, and defend ourselves if attacked, no more.

—This labor of yours—he begins.

—Ask no questions. It will be dangerous. It will take many weeks and involve much travel. When we're finished, I will free you from any obligation. Agree to this and I will ask Oda to return the sun. Do you agree?

Together they cry, Yes!

—From this time forth, you will obey me without question?

—Yes!

And so they do. Fine.

11
Noe

And the earth was corrupted before God, and was filled with iniquity.

GENESIS 6:11

People gather to laugh at him. A substantial crowd collects each morning in the shade of the hills behind his land: he can hear their whistles and jeers. Noe finds it inconceivable that anyone would bother to ride for days across scorching desert just for the sake of mocking him, but this appears to be what is happening.

Ribs from the ark jut skyward like the bones of some great beast. A whole series of them, fifty cubits apart, like splayed fingers, open hands, reach toward heaven at intervals of twenty cubits. Cross braces and scaffolding and interior decking have transformed the frame from a lifeless jumble of lumber into a web, an organic tangle that Cham and Sem and Japheth clamber through like spiders. Noe watches his sons at work, imperfect creations trying to achieve one perfect end, and his throat constricts. If he let himself, he'd flood his own beard with tears of pride.

But he does not let himself. He glances at the sky, which is void of clouds or overcast or vapor of any sort.

He stands and massages his neck, wondering how the girls are getting on with their animal collecting.

Within a few days it becomes apparent that the crowd gathered to jeer him has coalesced into a semi-permanent settlement. Lean-tos and shanties have sprung up like fungus, rickety structures in the lee of the hills. A steady population of perhaps thirty people has settled on the fringes of Noe's land, like a chancre. Their presence preys on his thoughts.

—Forget them, the wife advises.—We've got our hands full as it is.

She is right of course. But of course, it doesn't help. She squats among knee-high peas, snapping up finger-length pods and dropping them into her basket. Later she and Mirn will shell them and lay them on the roof to dry in the sun. The green mash the wife will eventually make of them is not Noe's favorite meal, but he knows it can keep them all alive.

—They bother me, Noe admits, speaking of the nonbelievers. He frowns as a waft of smoke from the smokehouse caresses his nose. Inside, salted oxflesh curls into chewy leather.—They are the Devil's tools.

The wife sighs. Sweat has collected in the bags under her eyes. She wears a pale red scarf which she now unties, shakes out and reknots.—You need to think about wood and pitch. We've little of one and none of the other.

—I guess I know all about that! he snarls, raking his beard.

—Then do something about it! she snaps back. Pointing

to the distant shanties:—Or they *will* have something to laugh about. Crazy Noe and the boat he never finished.

He's fuming but has no words. She's back to harvesting peas, turned away from him as if he's irrelevant.

Noe knows what he must do. It is not exactly the same as what he *should* do, which is to load his mule and ride north across the burning wasteland to beg more supplies off the giants. That would be the sensible thing. But Noe fears the journey, fears his own weakness in the face of it, and despairs of what he would say to the giants in any case.

So he does what he must do, which is walk through the olive grove to the shantytown.

The crowd is waiting for him, silent and expectant, when he arrives. They eye him. He eyes them back, knuckles aching where he clenches the staff.—Well?

No one speaks. They are an ordinary-looking crowd, mainly young men with a few old codgers and women. Their clothes are dusty and worn, their hair unkempt, but they are unremarkable enough. Well, what did he expect? Horns and forked tails, serpent tempters, angels with scorched wings?

Finally a short, thin man, so small that Noe had taken him for a child, speaks up.—We came to see your labor. You've grown quite famous, you know.

Some smirks at this among the crowd. A reedy-voiced, cross-eyed teenager calls out, It's not every day you see a ship growing in the desert.

Noe can barely restrain his trembling.—I have been called.

—Yeah, you been called lots of things, the boy says.

Everyone laughs.

—Have you forgotten God then? demands Noe.

A small-boned woman, curly-haired and pretty, steps before Noe.—Look around, old man. Seems to me that God has forgotten *you*.

—That's not true, Noe says petulantly.

—God threw Adam out of Paradise for eating an apple. Or so your story says. Does that sound like someone you should put your faith in?

More laughter, much nodding.

The woman lays a hand on his forearm.—Give up this fool's errand, and take some of what life offers. She unclasps her tunic and the cloth parts, revealing a plump, round body.—Rumor has it you've still got what it takes.

Noe shakes off her arm and steps back, but the crowd hoots and points at his erection, visible beneath his robes.—Stop this now! he cries at them.—You are the very reason God has grown wrathful! He is sending waters to drown you all, aye, and your parents and children too, and every living thing.

—Even the birds of the air and the fish in the sea? cries someone.

—Just so, even them! hollers Noe.

The half-naked harlot aims a crooked smile at him.—How can fish in the sea be drowned, when they're under water already?

Noe ignores her.—You can still repent. There is room for you in the boat, if you but choose to take it.

—What's your price? calls out an old man, stooped nearly parallel with the ground.—I've plenty of gold.

—Room on the vessel cannot be bought, Noe says, except with a pure heart.

The old man flutters his hand and turns away.

A stocky, tattooed man says, I'd rather barter for some of this. He hikes up the plump woman's tunic and ruts her on the ground in front of the crowd. The men form a circle, tugging themselves.

—I hope you can pay for this, the woman laughs over her shoulder. Her spherical backside judders with the man's thrusts.

The man's face contorts as he climaxes.—My daughter is nearly ten. You can have her.

—Agreed.

—If you can find her, the man adds amid much laughter.—I haven't seen her since my sister birthed her.

This is useless. Noe retreats, turns to go, but halts in mid-step as his eye falls on a curious sight. Some distance away lie two shimmering piles, coruscating in the sun like silver froth. Drawing closer, Noe squints in confusion until he realizes with a clench of his gut that he is seeing corpses, fairly fresh, covered as with fur by a shiny pelt of glittering blue flies. The smell hits him at the same moment. Breakfast rises burning in Noe's throat: he bites it back.

A man stands nearby, open-mouthed, staring at nothing. Noe demands of him, Why haven't these men been buried?

There is a softness to the man's face, as if God had deliberately avoided using straight lines in its design. The wet-lipped mouth opens fractionally wider. Genuine puzzlement flares up behind the droopy lids.—Bury them? Who'd do a thing like that?

—You for one.

The man blinks slowly.—Not me, uh-uh.

—It would be the decent thing to do. You can't just leave them here for the insects and the birds.

The man gazes stupefied at the piles.—They don't feel too bad about it I suppose.

Noe bites his lip, forcing down anger. He tries a different tack.—How did they die?

—Killed each other.

—Why?

—Fighting, I suppose.

Noe sighs long and hard through his nose.—What were they fighting about?

The man shuffles past him and peers intently at the bodies. Noe wonders briefly if he is being ignored, or if the man plans to question the dead. Instead, he reaches a soft hand into the dirt, rousing a cloud of blood-drunk flies. He gropes a moment, then lifts a small round pebble.—Over this.

Noe holds out his hand. Frowning, he takes the object and squints at it. A pearl, chipped along one face.—They murdered each other for this?

—Suppose so.

—Why?

The man's arms hang limp at his sides, like fish.—Both of them wanted it.

There is a lesson here for his children. Noe shakes his head and turns to go, but the man says, Hey. I want that.

—This? Noe holds up the pearl.—It's worthless.

The soft face has gone slack and feral.—Not to me, uh-uh.

—It doesn't belong to you.

—Not yours neither.

A sleek obsidian knife has appeared in the man's hand.—Don't make me kill you for it.

He would too, without hesitation. Never mind the fact that he could have taken the pearl any time since the fight.

Noe tosses the pearl at the man's feet.—God forgive you all.

—Not me, protests the man.—Uh-uh.

Noe flees the settlement as if pursued. Behind him men grunt as they rut the women, or the children, or each other. A fight has broken out: sticks pummel shrieking bodies. Crossing the orchard, Noe encounters a boy leading three tethered goats. Noe feels sure they are *his* goats. He stops the boy.—Where did you get those?

—Rut yourself, the boy spits, passing him.

He is too tired to argue anymore.—God save you.

—Rut Him too!

Noe staggers beneath an overwhelming sadness. The world is an ancient place, he knows, over a thousand years old: ten long centuries since Adam departed Paradise. Even so, it seems scarcely creditable that so much folly and depravity could have taken root and flourished so successfully, overwhelming the land like some demonic weed. How quickly mankind has forgotten God, Noe reflects. What then is the point of his labors? Surely all that is corrupt will simply swell up again, like a malign growth in the abdomen. If not in another thousand years, then in two, or three.

Noe casts his gaze skyward. His neck creaks. He frowns. The afternoon sun, falling westward, isn't quite as bright as it should be. In fact it is positively filtered. Discolored by some kind of haze. And low on the southern horizon, in the direction of the sea, thick dark clouds billow angrily toward him.

12
Japheth

So I'm up there with Cham, risking my neck to hold straight the framing timber for this great slab of a door we're trying to hang in the side of the boat, when your man comes tearing through the olives hollering like someone's just taken a handful of his almighty beard and stuck it in the fire. Which I'm halfway to wishing someone would, just once.

Charm hardly looks at me when he goes, What's the crisis?

—Rutted if I know.

Cham nods. One thing I like, he doesn't talk if there's nothing to say. Not like Sem or Da. Da talks a lot of crap and no mistake, but Sem's worse, if only because Sem says the same stuff as Da but not because he believes it, only because Da says he should. It's more than a body can put up with at times.

Of course Cham talks crap too sometimes and no mistake. But just now I have no argument when he goes, Might as well see what he wants.

We're twenty cubits off the ground so it takes a little climbing to get down. Which I don't mind, being fond of a little climbing. When we're on the ground at last, this stupendous half-built monster of a thing rears up above us. Like some skinless carcass blotting out half the sky, so long you can hardly see where it tails off in each direction. Say what you will about Cham, you have to admit he can knock a boat together.

Your man trots up to us all red and out of breath.— We must hurry, he goes.—Clouds are gathering. The rain'll start soon.

Cham goes, Small problem, Abba. No hull on the boat.

—Nor wood for it neither, I mention helpfully.

—And where are the animals? goes Cham.

—They're coming, goes your man with a certain touching vagueness.

—Bera and Ilya have been gone for weeks. You never should've sent them alone, Abba.

—There was no other way, he goes.

—You should've *found* another way.

They're set to go at it all afternoon, like they've done before. Fortunately for us all, I'm here, and I'm looking up at the sky.—Don't see no clouds, Da.

—Eh? he goes, looking up.—Oh. They're low. Follow me.

So he takes us round the other side of the boat and a long walk it is, hundred fifty cubits, just to look at the sky. We could've shortcutted through the ship, it's all open and unfinished, but neither of them think of it and why speak up? I don't mind a little break from the work. Mind you, I'm not one to complain, but my shoulders been killing me these past three weeks. Hacking boards and routing holes and knocking copper into nails will take it out of anybody. Not convinced? You try it.

We all stand there looking. Sure enough it's gone hazy to the south, the sun orange-red and angry, and there's a low line of dark stretching along the horizon. But none of it looks like clouds to me. Clouds would turn the sun silver, not red. I say as much.

Your man gapes at me.—Eh?

Cham's nodding though, right enough.—It's true, Abba. That's not a rain cloud. It's dust.

Once again I find myself impressed with Cham. Leaving home has really done wonders for him. He goes, There's either a dust storm coming up, or people on the way. Lots of people, judging from the size of that cloud.

—Wrong direction for a storm, goes your man.

—Yup.

He grunts then, picking at his beard like he's hunting for treasure. Isn't this interesting, thinks I. Visitors. A little luck, and we'll call it quits for the rest of the afternoon. Maybe I should go looking for Mirn, get a little something before the guests arrive.

No luck, though: Ma's alone in the eating room, slicing meat into strips for that Godawful smoked jerky. I go Ma, you seen Mirn? and she goes, She's out doing her collections.

Should've guessed. Mirn with her gourd boxes and urns. She could be anywhere.

—Anything to eat then Ma?

After a little while I notice that hazy cloud has gotten close, or anyway taller; it fills half the sky now, and the dark line along the horizon is starting to look very irregular and strange. So I finish my bread and cheese and go out to where your man and Sem and Cham are all standing at the edge of the western field, along the irrigation ditch, watching. Like they're some kind of I don't know what, welcoming committee. War party. Council of elders.

When I get there Sem's going, If it *is* her, she's not alone.

Count on Sem to state the obvious. I go, Her who? but they all ignore me.

Then Cham goes, Best wait and see.

Like this is a signal, Sem goes, I'm taking the mule, and hustles over to the pen.—Use your head, Cham calls after him, to no avail, and your man says nothing. Even I must admit to a certain queasiness, watching Sem mount up and ride off to meet that cloud.

In the end though it all works out okay. Close on sunset Sem comes trotting back, and in the fading light I can just make out a second rider behind him, dark like a shadow and who should it be but Princess Teats herself. Bera's not only managed to bring home the most scandalous assortment of creatures you could ever hope to lay eyes on, but she's got a couple of squalling babes on her lap, blacker even than she is and a hell of a lot noisier.

Adam's rib, thinks I. Next to me Cham has a perturbed look on his face, like he's weighing up the cargo and trying to figure whether the boat will take the stress. But your man there, next to him—why, my Da is absolutely beaming.

Such creatures there are as you've never seen in your life and count yourself lucky. But there's hardly time to take a proper look at any of them. Bera's jumping about, barking orders to put them in the lee of the mountains, or in amid the olives, or anyplace there's shade.—The heat is killing them, she goes.—Especially the big ones. Let's get them fed and watered.

For a time it's mayhem and no mistake. The afternoon is one of dust, a great shifting cloud of it that worms into my nostrils and eyeballs, kicked up by the lot of us as we hurry this way and that. Bera hasn't come back alone, you see. She's brought with her a black sour-faced gimp who loves nothing more than snapping orders that even she defers to. He's called "Captain" for some reason. Another half dozen strangers are with him, sullen and quiet, shiny with sweat and powdered with dust. Strong bastards all of them, who browbeat the animals and heave the cages into some kind of order. Maybe I didn't mention, all Bera's animals are in cages right enough, dozens of them, hundreds probably. And thousands of critters if you count the wild dogs and baby rodents and little monkeys no taller than your knee. Plus things unnamed and unknown, at least to me. These cages are stacked up on sleds of enormous timbers with runners underneath and pulled by teams of oxen and buffalo and camels and Yahweh knows what: big-haunched gray monsters with huge jutting teeth and noses that drag on the ground.—Adam's rib, is all I can mutter when I first set eyes on those bastards.

The one called Captain laughs at me and I say let him. I know when I'm in the presence of something mightier than myself. It happens during thunderstorms and earth tremors and clear nights with no moon, and here it's happening again right in front of me. I'd be stupid to say otherwise.

But it's not till the next morning, after I finish with Mirn and step outside to find Da and the others clumped together beside the boat, that I realize the extent of what Bera's brought us. Animals sure, plenty of them and no mistake. As for the newcomers, Bera's escort, they seem to have hived off. Bera herself has got her tunic hiked up and the babes planted on each teat, slurping away. Sem stares wide-eyed as if not sure whether to jump up and cheer, or go looking for his whetstone. Bera's been gone maybe two months and she was no more pregnant when she left than your man was, so it's clear these babes aren't Sem's. He seems to have been burdened with the task of fathering them now, however.

From the olive grove comes a grunting murmur like a wind through the trees, only there's no wind, or the ocean against the rocks, except there's no ocean and precious few rocks. It's the sound of a couple thousand bodies waking up and stretching, hocking and rutting and farting. A couple thousand creatures wondering what'll happen today that didn't happen yesterday. Not so different from me. Or you.

Cham turns to Da and goes: Abba, do you see those sleds Bera brought?

—Indeed I do, goes your man.

—I've an idea how we could put them to good use.

—Do you now? And Da looks over and—I'm not lying—*winks*. This is not typical behavior. He goes, I'd say it's about enough to hull the boat.

—It'll make a good start, goes Cham.—Might be enough. Might not.

—Praise Yahweh, goes Da, sort of whistling through his teeth. But when I look over at him he's not staring at the timber sleds, or even the animals in their cages. He's got his eyes fixed on Bera and the twerps, and Sem is looking at him, frowning and nodding at the same time. As if he isn't sure whether things are how they're supposed to be, or if they've gotten unaccountably skewed when he wasn't around to keep an eye out. But he seems willing to accept Da's judgment on the matter. Like the good son that he is.

13
Noe

Some days later, Noe announces to his family in the eating room: If I am not mistaken, this morning there truly *are* clouds.

Everyone tumbles outside. Thin herringbone nimbus fling themselves toward every horizon. Japheth hoots and punches the air. Sem glances at Bera, who stands impassive. Cham sighs heavily with hands on hips. Mirn giggles. Noe's wife wrinkles her nose and returns to the kitchen, from where she calls, Food's getting cold.

They settle in a ragged oblong around the cookfire. For a time they eat silently as if sobered. Finally Sem asks, How long do you think we have?

Noe frowns and tugs his beard.—As much as we need. Cham, how long till the hull is ready?

Cham says nothing.

Noe clears his throat.

Cham says nothing.

—Cham?

—Find me some rutting pitch! he snarls at his

father.—And don't say a word about leaving till Ilya's back.

With this Cham rises and storms from the room, food limp on his plate.—The giants agreed to bring it, Noe sighs to his family.—They're late but there's little I can do. I've explained this to Cham but it appears I must do so again.

—Bad idea that, Japheth grunts.

—He's right, puts in the wife.—Just let him be.

They arrive that afternoon, six of them bearing leather sacks the size of granaries. Hot pitch overflows, sloppy and sticky and adhering quickly to whatever it touches. Noe watches as the giants kick out hollows in the dirt alongside the boat, then deposit the skins inside them. Wordlessly they disappear over the horizon to the north. Noe knows their timely arrival is yet another miracle. He knows he should fall prostrate, speechless, bawling before God. But there have been many miracles already, and he is bone tired.

—Forgive me, Lord, he stammers silently.—Your vessel is imperfect, but I do the best I can.

His neck throbs as the clouds thicken. His back twinges, as do his molars on the left side and his instep on the right. Lately he is constipated, and he sometimes forgets things. There will be time later for gratitude. He hopes. For now he sends Bera to cut horsetails for brushes, and assigns Mirn campfire duty to keep the pitch warm and viscous. Then they all get busy slapping tar onto the interior of the hull. They labor in near-blackness, the only light admitted by the chinks and cracks they are endeavoring to obliterate. From time to time they emerge like newborn pups, like chicks from an egg, to swap brushes and gulp clean air. Through it all, Cham is silent as a knife.

The work is pitiless. The heat inside the ship desiccates them as well as any smokehouse. Late in the afternoon Cham throws down his brush and announces, Inside's finished. Time to quit.

—We're nearly done, Noe protests, following him out into the light, blinking furiously.

—We're nearly done *in*, Cham corrects.—We've still got to do the outside. Which'll have to wait a couple days.

Noe squints skyward.—No point tempting fate.

Cham says, You think your God would wash us away so close to being done?

—Don't blaspheme, Noe warns.—And he's your God too.

—Just asking.

Sem, nervously:—Why don't we go ahead and finish now, Cham? Then it's done.

Cham sighs.—The inside needs to dry first.

No one speaks.

—Meanwhile, we can decide how to organize the cargo.

—Organize? asks Sem. His eyes flicker to Noe, who licks his lips with the expression of an old man wrestling a new idea.

—Oh for God's sake! Cham croaks, and strides toward the house. Japheth trots after, as if eager to quit work. Sem shrugs apologetically and says to Noe, I guess he's right, Father. After all you put him in charge.

Summoning what he can of his dignity, Noe nods.

—Of course. He's correct, we need to discuss the uh the ahh—

—The cargo?

Noe grunts. To be honest he hasn't quite thought the problem through, though he would never allow the others to catch on to that fact.

For days after, clouds clot the sky like blood.

Noe gathers his family and says, I have given much thought to how to organize the animals on the ship. I propose that we follow God's natural order. As humans created in the image of God, we shall inhabit the top deck of the craft, along with the apes and other two-legged creatures. Below us, in the middle deck, shall be the animals with four legs. Worms and serpents, insects and other abominations, whether multi-limbed or altogether legless, shall be left to the bottommost reaches.

Japheth shrugs.—All right then, that's settled.

Sem is frowning, but it is Cham who speaks.—That's preposterous. Those huge monsters out there, the what do you call them? Elephants, hippos and whatnot? We can't have them amidships, they'll make the boat more unstable than it already is. Which is bad enough, he adds.

Noe blinks.—I see.

An awkward lull ensues, everyone waiting as if for judgment. Sem pokes his wife, who is gazing hard at the floor.—What do you think, Bera? You brought them. How would you arrange them?

She blinks as if preoccupied.—Hmm? Oh, color, I suppose. Brown and gray on the bottom, yellow and orange in the middle, black and white on top. Red in the front and blue in the back. Is anything blue?

No one can remember if there is anything blue.

—Anyway, Bera goes on, you can do it the other way round, if you prefer.

Noe stares with mouth open as if wondering at her sanity.—Birds too? You'd put the orange birds in with the orange wild cats and orange snakes?

Japheth laughs.—And orange monkeys, Da. Orange butterflies.

—You asked, shrugs Bera.—That's my thought.

From the window floats a lilting voice.—As ever, an interesting one, sister. Just not too practical.

Chaos ensues, not formless or void, but bewildering nonetheless. Cham out the door, Ilya in his arms. Everyone else on his feet, Japheth laughing, Mirn chattering merrily, Noe's wife scurrying for some bread and stew to offer. For some reason a sheep has gotten underfoot and is bleating.

—Abba, come outside, calls Cham in a voice that drops through the excitement like a mallet.—Our job just got a touch more difficult.

14
Mirn

Ilya has *lots* of animals and I don't like them much. They're all big furry boring ferocious things. Foxes and wolves, big-antlered deer and bears. Lots of bears, black and brown and yellow-white, and all of them in a bad mood, all the time. Ho-hum.

The men with Ilya are as scary as the animals, and about as furry and fierce. They don't stay long, which makes me happy. Ilya sends them away the next morning, *commands* them to go! They seem glad enough to leave.

The animals are like prisoners tied in long lines of double-woven rope. The bigger bears and wolves wear orange metal collars and their fur is eaten away, showing skin underneath, pink and raw. I feel sorry for them when I see that. We put them all in the shade and then Papa's having his big meeting again about how they should go in the boat. It's so boring I want to cry. Papa says again to arrange them according to their closeness to God, which leaves *every*one confused, not just me. Bera says to do it by color, which is just dumb. Sometimes Bera says things that make me wonder what it is she thinks about so much.

Then Ilya says to do it by classification of animal, and when we all look blank she goes on about egg-laying and live births, and nest-builders and den-diggers, and lizards and insects and furry animals. Every time I think I understand what she's getting at, she snatches it away and changes it and adds something that leaves me ready to cry I'm so confused. So I slip away from them all and go out past the mustard field and into the little ravine with the creek and past the rocky pool and the little water-fall to where the ground gets marshy. I bring some clay pots for collecting. Under a flat round rock I find a red millipede as long as my *arm*, and a bunch of little brown beetles with ridged shells. Nearby are some blue-and-yellow grasshoppers on the long grass, not green like I usually find so I take them too and some leaves for them to eat, and a bunch of worms. There are little green frogs that smile at me and go cheepeep, and a pink newt that I catch then lose then catch again. And snails and things. It's not long before I've got the pots practically overflowing. I see plenty of crickets and caterpillars and other things but I've got lots of them already. I take some caterpillars anyway, since I can never have *too many*.

When I get back to the house the others are still talking. I add my new things to the collection I already have, take out the dead ones which actually aren't that many, and go back for some spiders I noticed at the far end of the mustard.

And later they're *still* at it. Arguing about this and that but it's not a real argument where people *listen* and maybe change their minds about things. It's the kind of argument where everyone is actually saying, This is what I think and I'm not going to listen to what you say because that would be like admitting I'm *wrong*.

Then everyone stops talking. I say, Do it by size.

—Hush, says J., but Papa says, Eh? at the same time.

It's so obvious. I tell them, Put the big things on the bottom with the little things on top and the medium things in between. If you put the little things in with the big things then the big things will eat the little things or crush them and the medium things won't know how to act and will get confused.

I stop. I don't like talking to everyone this way but they're all fussing so much. Anyway Papa's nodding.—God speaks through this child, he says.

It makes me happy to think something like that.

Even Cham who scares me when he's so grumpy all the time says: That'll help in balancing the boat. Provided of course all those heavy animals don't punch holes through the bottom.

That's just the way Cham is. He can't say anything good without saying something gloomy too. Though maybe he'll be better now Ilya's back.

For a while then they talk about this but I know it's just talk. My way makes sense: little things like being with little things, that's why they're always together. Turn over a rock and find what? A bunch of little things. Is there a horse under there? No.

That night in bed J. grabs my fanny.—Such a smart girl.

—Well it was obvious.

—Sure it was, he says, and his thing goes in me.—
That's why nobody else thought of it.

—People never pay attention to *little* things, I whisper,
but he's not listening.

The next two days no one talks about anything but the
weather. Ho-hum. The whole sky is covered with flat gray
clouds like a roof. The men hurry to finish tarring the
boat, and when it's done it's the biggest thing I've ever
seen except for the world. Standing at one end with J. at
the other, I can hold up my thumb and cover his whole
body like he's not even *there*. Now it's all black with tar
and shiny like a huge burnt log left behind some gigantic
cookfire.

Once it's done the men stand around not knowing
what to do. They stare at the sky so much I wonder if
they see something I can't. Meanwhile Mama and the rest
of us have our hands full getting provisions ready for the
boat. We've done a good job, according to Mama. Lots
of stores are already loaded aboard, but since nobody knows
how long we'll be afloat and how much food we'll need,
she's never satisfied or relaxed.

I sneak away when I can. Collecting is harder now
that I'm running out of containers, they're all being used
for dates and olives and cheese and oil. But I make do.
It's amazing how many tiny creatures there are out there,
and God made them all. Sometimes I wonder why He
bothered, since most people never even see them. Or if
they do see they *hate* them, like snakes. People call snakes

the Devil's lackeys but I think, Okay, there was *one* bad one but not all of them. So I catch a bright green one with a lumpy head and yellow stripes all down his throat, lazy with just having eaten. He sticks his tongue out at me but that's not scary. I pop him in my sack along with the other two I've found today. They all squirm and go sssss but I know they don't mean anything by it. Most people I know would say worse things than sssss if somebody put *them* in a sack.

It's after dinner now. The others have all gone to the sleeping room and I know J. is waiting for me with his thing. I'll go soon, but dusk is a good time for collecting with the animals being out and restless and the chores done for the day. So I take my snake sack and tiptoe over the long grass to where I hear some rustling. Something's creeping low to the ground—a mouse or vole? Or a lizard. It doesn't sound like a snake. I lean forward, squinting into the dimness but using my ears really. I'm like a bat. Whatever it is goes tick-tick-tick then stops. Something brushes my shoulder but I ignore it.

There! It's a vole all right, frozen under the grass. I take another sneaky step. Something taps my cheek, some bug probably. I wave it away. Where's that vole gone? Disappeared somehow, heard me coming. My footsteps are like thunder to these little ones.

Something nips my nose then, then my shoulder, my forearm, my other shoulder, and I realize these aren't bugs. I forget about the vole and race back to the house, hollering all the way.

—Get *up*, it's raining! *Raining!*

There's a commotion in the house but they're awful slow to get moving.

—I just felt another drop!

All at once they come pouring out of the house, and stare at the sunset-purple clouds. Rain clouds. Drops are coming thicker now. Everybody looks at everybody else, then up at the sky again. Inside the sack the snakes snap their bodies back and forth like lashes.

Far away there's thunder, tripping around the sky in a circle. Like the footsteps of a giant who's trying to sneak up on us.

PART TWO
RAIN

I
Mirn

Went in to Noe into the ark, two and two of all flesh,
wherein was the breath of life.

GENESIS 7:15

It's like being a little creeping thing inside a big dark hollow
log full of other little creeping things. Cramped and stinky
and hardly any light to see by. The smell of tar fights with
wet fur and dung from the animals. I guess they're scared.
They're all going moo baa grunt squeak growl. Everything's *damp*, inside and out, the desert giving off a surprised
wet-sand smell and the rain coming on thicker now. It's
still more a shower than anything else, the thunder holding
off to the south. Hard to believe it'll amount to much. But
it's enough to make us notice our clothes and even our
own *skin*, the way we don't most other times.

Moving about is hard. For such a big boat there's not
much room to walk around. I'm glad I'm small. Poor Cham
keeps knocking into the walls and swearing, and Sem bumps
his head every time he goes through a doorway. Hi Sem
thump Bye Sem. He doesn't swear but I can tell he wants
to. Mostly everyone is just clumsy with not knowing where
things are and with the animals everyplace. The special

ones we get into their places okay, big to little, bottom to top just like I said. But there's goats and ducks and chickens that we haven't got to putting in their pens as yet, there's just so much to do, and they keep popping up in the oddest places. You reach for a ladder and your hand comes down on something *furry*. Outside on the upper deck there are no animals but it's raining, so that's not exactly comfortable either.

It doesn't help that it's night. Cham says we must be careful with the torches because of the pitch, so there are only a few lanterns. The ones on the deck sputter in the rain like they're angry. Going back below again is like jumping into a cave.

Somehow though we get most of the animals inside. They come quietly enough, just sort of plonking down where we lead them. It's not till they're inside that they start bickering with one another. J. and Sem and Papa are bringing the last ones now while Cham walks around the boat with a lamp, checking for leaks, and Ilya and Bera carry in the silage for the grazing animals. Their shadows flood through the hallways in weird shapes, long heads and arms like wings and fingers like claws, as if the animals we've brought weren't bad *enough*. Underfoot the little ones scurry and slither and hop with shining eyes.

The rain rattles against the boat like a drum. Once when I was a little girl I went with my parents to the cascades on the far side of the mountains. This was before Mama died and Papa started staying awake every night counting stars until he cried. Before J. came with *his* papa, who's my papa now, and said that J. would marry me and take care of me and my real papa cried some more and said okay. At the cascades, my *real* mama and papa set me under a rock overhang beneath the waterfall where I could hear it crashing down. It was like being inside a bell. Now, standing here under the deck of the boat and listening to the rain pelting out of the dark with strange animals all round me and the smell of tar in my nose, that memory comes back so *strong* that I almost get the feeling that my parents are *here with me*. Their spirits or whatever, and then I wonder if it's a sin to think like that. Probably, the way it makes me feel, with my forearms prickled up and me sure that someone's behind me when no one is.

Maybe it's God in the boat with us. Papa says God is in everything and especially living things. If that's true then there must be an awful lot of God in snails and ants and leeches and spiders and locusts and crickets and moths. But I don't know how it works exactly. Does a cow have more God in it than an ant? Do a million ants have more God than a cow? And what about *people*—does a person have more God in him than one of Ilya's bears, even though a bear is so much bigger? Or does everything have the same amount? I think that's what makes the most sense, otherwise it's like trying to fit God into one of Mama's recipes. Two parts of God in a chicken, twenty in a person, fifty in a camel and one-thousandth in a skink. That's crazy.

But if it's all the *same* amount of God in everything then we shouldn't eat cows or pigs or chickens. Because then we're eating God! Or kill ants, which I don't, actually, but everybody else does. From the way people act, it's easy to see they don't think God is in everything, not really. Just in *them*. But that's so dumb it makes me want to cry. Just look at a beehive sometime, the way they all fuss to build their little rooms just so and dance to tell each other where the flowers are. Or watch two snakes mating, or a spider spinning its web. How can God *not* be in that? A person has to be *blind* to miss it.

When I ask Papa these things he smiles at me and puts his hand on my head. That's what he does when he thinks I'm dumb or else he can't answer the question. Ho-hum.

Lately what Papa says is that God is angry and is going to destroy the whole world except us. I should feel sad about that but I don't. It shows that I was right all along, that we're all *equal*, ants and mice and human beings and worms. Just a few of each will survive, and the ones that will live are the things we save. The little things I've collected will be safe, they'll lay eggs and hatch and crawl out to cover the earth. The worms will go into the ground and the moths will come out at night and the salamanders will live by the ponds. I like thinking about how it will all happen because of *me*. It's the sin of pride to think that way but I can't help it. Only Yahweh can create life, that's true, but I've been able to save a little bit of it from being destroyed. That's pretty good, for a person. It's about the best thing that a human being could ever hope to do.

2
Noe

Dawn creeps in like a bad idea. The sky lightens incrementally, revealing ever drearier shades of gray. Clouds jostle each other, spilling water into thirsty sand that slurps it up and begs for more. It has rained much of the night, but this morning's landscape, though soggy, is not drowned.

There is no flood.

Noe stands at the rail of the boat surrounded by his family and a few dozen perplexed birds. The ark stretches away on all sides, so immense as to beggar belief, like God. It sits square-ended, flat-bottomed, an enormous pitch-smeared box. At the moment, it remains stubbornly attached to the ground.

The birds arrived in the night in ones and twos, refugees seeking asylum. Now they twitch their tail feathers against the raindrops and cheep questions to one another.

Nobody else says much. Everyone is on deck except Cham, who prowls the lower decks seeking structural faults.

From the impromptu shanty village at the far end of

the olive grove, a few figures wend close enough to call out. Their words are indistinct but the gist is clear. Rain has materialized, deluge has not. Noe is a fool. Noe is a lunatic. Noe hears voices that no one else hears, and sees things that aren't there. And who is crazier: the crazy man or the people who put their faith in him?

Sem clears his throat as if embarrassed, as if planning to ask a question, but falls silent again.

Cham hoists himself through the hatch in the deck, bearing a small olive-oil lamp. His face is smudged and his beard carries tangles of straw.—No leaks as yet, he tells them.—She seems to be holding up.

—Good, says Noe.

—Of course, there are some compartments I didn't inspect too closely. Cham shakes his head and squints at Bera.—Some of those creatures you brought back, woman. My God. Who thought them up?

Bera smiles mysteriously.—Ask your father.

Cham shakes his head again, eyeing the hatch.—Crazy stuff down there, he says with a grimace. Then, taking in the birds around him, he asks, Who brought these?

—Nobody, Mirn explains.—They just showed up.

Cham grunts softly. As he watches, a pair of orioles flutters onto deck, male and female, twinned flashes of black-orange. They stretch their necks toward their fellows—crows, thrushes, owls—and chirp experimentally.

—Makes you wonder if they know something we don't, murmurs Cham.

3
Japheth

So we're standing there on this great rutting monster, going nowhere in a hurry. All these people down there, laughing up at us. They're wet as we are but at least they're enjoying themselves. A proper party they've got going, wine and women too if my eyes don't deceive me. Sure, we're paying the price for their fun. Rutting Noe and his half-baked schemes. We'll be hearing about this for years and no mistake.

Down below you can hear all the snorts and snuffles of the animals we've just spent the night loading aboard, the growls and roars and screeching, and some merry music it is too. Meanwhile around us are so many birdies we can hardly take a step without pinching feathers between our toes.

I can't say as that I'm too pleased about recent developments, no I'm not. If it's going to flood, then flood already. If not, well, I've got business to take care of, things to do, a wife to rut.

Which is when I shoot a glance at your man and get

a bit of a shock: he's smiling. Now my Da's not partial to smiling, or in fact giving away much of any emotion except maybe a certain crusading glumness, so seeing this particular toothy grin clawing its way past the beard is a bit like hearing a goat say Excuse me, could you direct me to the nearest spring? He's got his arms thrown open wide like to embrace the rain, and his face up to the clouds and Whoever might be on the other side of them. His eyes are screwed tight shut but you can tell, the way his head's trembling, he's having a mighty conversation with *something*.

Then in a whoosh he drops to his knees and comes out with: I thank Thee, O Lord.

Around him the birdies all flutter startled into the air, then settle again.

One thing I'll say for your man, when he gets going with Yahweh it's hard to stare him down or laugh him off. You'd understand if you ever heard that voice, or saw that maniac look of his. So it's not such a surprise that we all go down alongside, thump thump thump, knees into planks right there in the drizzle. Even Cham, who's usually as slow at these things as me, and my Mirn, who I half suspect of living in her daydreams most of the time.

—O Lord, goes Da, deliver us this day from our enemies who would disparage us, and our labor, and through us, You. Deliver us, yea, and smite them unto silence.

Take that, you bastards, thinks I.

—We stand ready to do your will, O Lord. We have done as you commanded. We have built this your ark, and collected all that which lives upon the earth. For the rest, we submit ourselves unto Your divine will. Amen.

—Amen, goes Sem.

—Amen, goes Bera and Ilya and Mirn and even Cham. Only Ma's looking at the hatch Cham left open, as if wondering whether she should go close it to keep the water out.

—Amen, I mutter, and look overhead. The rain comes and comes and no mistake, maybe a trifle heavier now. Clouds look like they're getting the idea to stick around awhile. It occurs to me that we might indeed be in for some serious weather.

Then something trembles, reaching up through the deck and rattling our knees where we've dropped onto the boards. Almost as if the earth itself is settling a bit, the boat shifting where she heels in the mud. There it is again, that juddering. A sideways-slipping kind of feeling, and last night's dinner sloshes about in my stomach most unpleasantly. I'm not overly fond of boats, I decide, though I realize this might not be the best of times to make that particular confession.

Though when would be a good time for it? This I ask in all seriousness. And when the boat slippy-slides again, I must admit to a certain icy apprehension.

At least we'll have a Hell of a story to tell the grandkids, thinks I.

4
Noe

And the flood was forty days upon the earth, and the waters increased, and lifted the ark on high from the earth.

GENESIS 7:17

Six days later, surrounded by birds, Noe watches the water. Rain pelts down like God's judgment, which it is. Gray-black clouds bruise the sky; the world all around is rinsed into gray and white and pale aquamarine, as if endless water has leached all color from the palette of creation.

Never has Noe felt so alive.

Amid the tempest, the ark floats. It has been borne on the water since that first morning, when it was lifted roughly by the irresistible tide and heaved backwards, a leaf into a flume.

Noe squints. Around him the floodscape heaves with a geography all its own. Mountains rise and fall, valleys open and collapse, continents collide in huge tectonic spasms. The ark rides these upheavals like a pelican, stung at times by spray but managing to hurl itself over the next swell.

Still the rain falls. Empty barrels, lashed into the corners of the deck to collect rainwater, were half-full after the first day and overflowing ever since. Noe has commanded that more be brought on deck, to take advantage of God's bounty.

At first he had trouble keeping his balance on the convulsing deck, writhing under his feet like a thing possessed. Now he barely registers the movement, his fist-sized calves clenching and unclenching, knees buckling in turn to keep him upright. Bare bony feet cling for purchase to the rough-wet tar.

There is not much to look at, but Noe looks anyway. Mainly he sees water. He is soaked to the bone and expects to remain so for some time. Skin peels from his fingers like pennants, and an angry pink rash scars his torso. Noe feels it not. Winds howl, but he barely notices: he is enveloped in a mantle of supernatural warmth.

The birds around him share no such contentment. They cluster miserably, crows and jays, larks and finches, sparrows and rollers and doves: a multidenominational carpet of plumage stretching the length and breadth of the deck. A sorrier bunch of living things would be difficult to conceive. They are uninvited guests at the worst party ever, feathers fluffed out against the spray and rain and incessant wind.

Angels soar overhead, riding the currents, casting their beneficent gaze downward. The birds don't react as the angels shower Noe with a kind of holy serenity that leaves him teary. He waves in silent appreciation and they nod in return before whisking off.

Noe tingles from scalp to fingertips to toes. He is consumed by an acute energy, even giddiness, and his perceptions seem preternaturally clear: every foaming whitecap imprints itself on his vision, every angelic wingstroke. Perhaps this is due to water and wind and simple organic physiology, perhaps the birds around him tingle from beak to talons and are quietly enjoying it. But maybe not: standing beneath the smile of God has consequences. Perhaps his forehead burns with righteousness, not fever.

The wife is having none of it. She has materialized beside him, small but determined, rugged in a way Noe has never seen before. She is matter to Noe's spirit. Pushing a bowl of stew into his hands, she uses her own to bracket his face. Her eyes, green as lichen, are heavy with concern.—You're burning up. You've got to come below.

Noe looks into the bowl. Rain peppers his lunch, but the food doesn't appeal to him.—I'm fine.

—Don't be a fool.

Noe gazes benignly at the wife. She has been a good companion, dutiful and patient. He feels himself inclined to forgive her occasional shrewishness, then silently thanks God for his magnanimity.—All right, he says with a twinkle, I won't be a fool. What do you want me to do?

She taps the bowl.—Eat that. Then come below and get dried off, and rest.

—I'll just get wet again later.

—Better still if you dry off first and then eat, but I'll not ask for miracles.

Noe takes a placating mouthful. It's gone cold in the rain but tastes nourishing anyhow.—Look about you. You're living a miracle.

The wife's mouth is one wrinkle among many.—If this is a miracle, I'd hate to see catastrophe.

—A catastrophe is this boat capsizing.

She falls silent at that. A big swell crunches into the hull, rocking them alarmingly as if to prove Noe's point. He continues eating as the boat steadies and the wife stands with her arms crossed, showing perhaps that she can bear anything he chooses to. He appreciates the gesture, but there is little point exposing the woman to needless hardship. If there is such a thing, wonders Noe, then decides that's a puzzle for another day.

He drains his bowl and says, No harm going below for a time, I suppose.

—First sensible thing you've said in days.

Smiling indulgently, Noe follows her below.

Hell is something like this, he thinks.

The smell alone is enough to send him outside again: the stench of dung both animal and human, the stale six-day-old air choked by the wife's cookfire and the over-heated bodies of all creation. Other layers add spice to the miasma: Japheth's acid vomit, the cats' urine.

His family, themselves vomit-colored, sprawl in the little bulkhead compartment near the bow. A row of small square windows lets in too little light and air and too much rain and spray. In one corner Japheth writhes and curses. Sem holds Bera's head in his lap: her eyes remain fixed on the beams overhead as she clutches her two infants. Ilya and Cham occupy themselves in resolutely collecting buckets of dung from the holds below, clambering up the ladder to the deck, and dumping the waste overboard. It is an endless job. Next to one of the windows, the wife tends a tippy cookstove. Noe shudders: one solid wave would pitch those coals into the tar, and thus would his holy calling come to an end. But the family must eat, and for that a fire is needed. At least some of the smoke is drawn out the window, although some—too much—gusts back inside.

Only Mirn seems unaffected. She sits with an armful of yellow chicks, which spill away from her and caper in frantic circles. Mirn laughs and dives to catch and collect them on her lap, where they rest a moment before scampering off again.

Sweat limns Noe's face. Air that is damp and cool outside is hot and marshy here. The jolts and rocking of the ship, unnerving enough abovedecks, are magnified in this place, and he feels his knees buckle and his stomach flutter. Bent suddenly like an old man, he lurches to the bulkhead, lowering himself to the deck. Something protests. Startled, he jolts up and watches an indignant duck waddle off, honking irritably. Noe checks beneath him and drops to the deck once more. Rough boards spit splinters into his flanks. Maybe it is the foul air, or the relentless swinging of the boat, but suddenly he is not experiencing the beneficent smile of God anymore. Nor do angels inhabit this cabin. His vision turns watery and he closes his eyes, slipping into vertiginous dreams of blinding colorless light and the infinite, unfathomable vortex.

5
Ilya

And all flesh was destroyed that moved upon the earth, both
of fowl, and of cattle, and of beasts, and of all creeping
things that creep upon the earth: and all men.

GENESIS 7:21

The frightening thing wasn't so much the rain or the flood,
or even those poor people drowning like rats. Though that
was horrible enough, of course—the destruction of the
known world isn't anything a sane person can look upon
without terror. But what left me truly cold, genuinely
afraid, was Noe's reaction to it all. Which was, in a word,
jubilation.

I have learned very quickly that he's not a typical father-
in-law. Noe plays by his own rules and a person either goes
along with them or gets out of the game. Fine. I went
along. I even went and brought home some animals, at no
small risk to myself, though I've spoken of this to no one.
Astonishingly, no one has asked about it, not even Cham.
Nor about Bera's journey as far as I know. But then they're
a self-absorbed lot, I understood that very quickly indeed.

To be honest, when the rain started I was shocked. I
had supposed my father-in-law to be something of a

crackpot, though admittedly a compelling one. I never expected him to be right.

But he was.

The crowd of unbelievers broke up early that first morning, went off to their huts to do whatever it is that unbelievers do. Did. The rain kept on. By mid afternoon the barrels on deck were one-third full—that's a cubit of water in less than a day—and the ship was listing perceptibly as the ground beneath it became saturated. Puddles formed ankle-deep in the furrows of the mustard field. We had an uneasy time belowdecks that first night, the cabin cramped and smoky. When morning finally came it brought a view of knee-high water across the land, flat like a mirror pocked with raindrops, reflecting the tarnished-silver sky. The water barrels were two-thirds full.

There was a crowd alongside the boat then all right, whining and hollering to get on, holding their children overhead. Noe's answer was predictable.—You had your chance, he barks at them.

So they did, but still. I couldn't help but reflect on the events that had brought me to this pass—starting with my mother's death when I was a child. Later I was allowed to accompany my father on his travels, acquiring, as a result, the rudiments of a dozen coastal languages. When he died in a wreck off the Kittim, my chance encounter with Cham was able to develop—falteringly, and with many misunderstandings—into something more. Thus we married. Change any of those circumstances, and I'm not on this boat. I'm down there in the crowd, pleading, Don't leave me here to die.

It is a feeling of vulnerability which my father-in-law has evidently forgotten, or perhaps never experienced.

Noe heckled the crowd, You can explain yourselves to Yahweh.

Well, yes. But need you be so smug about it? I swear he smacked his lips as if savoring their anguish.

I said, Maybe there's room for some of the little ones.

He turned that icy glare on me.—It's not your place to make that offer. You are not to judge.

—And you are? I snapped back, before I could rein myself in.

—Yahweh decides, he answered with perfect calmness.

—What about the children?

His eyes were like blue coals.—We shall have children enough of our own.

Fine. So on top of everything else, the fact of my childlessness—of Cham's and my childlessness—was oozing to the surface. Maybe Bera would let me have one of those babes she'd found or bought or dug up from under a log or whatever.

Not likely.

That's when I noticed the rumble. First I thought it was the rain coming on heavier, or the wind picking up. Then I realized it was the bellow of thunder and then, moments later, realized it wasn't. I ran to the hatch to call for Cham but he was halfway up the ladder already, Mirn behind him and the others following. They welled up out of the hatch like blood, swirling in the rain, trying to locate the source of the roar.

Noe pointed. The western horizon was a thick dark

line. As we watched, it grew thicker. Darker. Taller.

—God in Heaven! Cham yelled, furious.

The boat pointed west so the water—this wall of water, this inundation, tidal wave, deluge, whatever—would slam us head-on. I realize now that's just as well. If it had hit lengthwise, we'd have rolled like a log, shattering and powdering like eggshells. Still it was terrifying to stand clustered at the bow of the boat as that disaster sprinted toward us. Rollers of dirty foam and silvery streaks of light flashed where it wrenched upward.

Cham's hand whirled me around. His face was frenzied.—Get below!

—But—

The first and last time he ever touched me with anything other than exquisite tenderness was when he hurled me back toward the hatch.—Don't argue!

Of course he was right. The water rushed on like a towering wall taller than the boat. It wasn't, but we didn't know that then. Perspective plays funny tricks on the eyes, and so does fear. For all we knew the water would sweep us off the deck like sand before a broom. So we all of us bolted to the hatch, when I heard a faraway shriek and remembered those poor people down below.

I couldn't help myself. I ran to the rail and looked over. God help me, I wish I hadn't. I'd never before seen the faces of thirty-odd souls who knew they would die within moments, and I hope I never do again.

Cham's hand on my shoulder.

I looked up. The water seemed close enough to touch.

The roar was such that Cham had to bellow in my ear:
For pity's sake, Ilya, get below.

And even as I dropped down the ladder, my mind
spun like a dog chasing its tail. Why me, and not them?
Why them, and not me?

I feared there was no good answer.

Belowdecks was a fraction quieter but a great deal more
crowded. Fear was so heavy in the air we tripped over it.
Japheth in particular was babbling some hysterical nonsense and briefly I was glad of the noise outside.

When the water hit we all stopped worrying about
the noise for a while. An almighty *thwack* shot through
the length of the boat, and a lurch upward left my
stomach behind for a few moments. Then my stomach
caught up with me and kept wanting to go up while the
rest of me crashed back down. This went on for some
time.

Somehow I found myself lying prone, wedged into a
corridor that led down to the livestock pens. Over the rain
and waves I heard the racket the animals made. My fingers
came to rest on something small and furry, and I realized
Mirn's head was in my lap. She lay motionless until I said,
Are you all right?

—I think so, she answered calmly.—Are we floating?

—I believe so.

—We're not sinking?

—Not as far as I know.

—That's good then. Is Papa all right or did he get
washed overboard?

That made me wonder. I sat up.—Let's go see.

On deck Noe and Sem were leaning into each other, staring at I don't know what. There wasn't a great deal to stare at, just water and the tops of a few tall trees and a swirling eddy or two. Though admittedly there was something compelling about all that destruction—it held one's attention the way fire does, an endless devouring. Bits of jetsam everywhere, thatch from roofs, fence posts, drowning roosters, that sort of thing. The water more brown than blue, rolling with foam. Falling behind us as we drifted, the hills behind the farm stood half-drowned.

Sem greeted me with, Where's Cham?

I shrugged.—Down below, perhaps. Checking for leaks.

Sem nodded. Noe said, with mystic calm, There are none.

Yes, well. I said, It's a wonder you didn't get washed away.

—Many are the miracles of Yahweh, said Noe.

—Also, the water wasn't so high, put in Sem.—Only maybe twenty cubits. Enough to lift the ship without swamping it.

Noe shot him a look.

—Which was miraculous in itself, mumbled Sem.

Beneath our feet, the deck swooped and lurched. I hoped this would settle down soon, but suspected it might not. Rain continued slashing diagonally and there wasn't a chink to be seen in the thunderheads. I asked, Those poor people who were on the ground?

—What about them? spat Noe.

—They drowned, I suppose?

—Praise God, I hope so, he murmured. Hesitantly, Sem nodded agreement.

—That's disgusting, I said.

Noe turned his gaze on me. He had the kind of look that said, If you want to join them, I'm happy to help. What he said out loud was, They were sinners.

—So are we all, I reminded him.

—They were unclean in the sight of the Lord, he pushed on.—A stain that needed to be cleansed. Old is this world, a thousand years or more. It had grown heavy with filth and weary with sin. Now it has been scrubbed clean.

The old man was beaming out at the water, at the cleansing waves, scrubbing away. Joy illumined every line of his face. My stomach heaved, and it wasn't solely due to the bucking of the deck.

—Men.

His smile wavered as he looked at me.

—Only a man could call a child filth. No woman could look on a dead infant and feel such happiness.

—Ilya, said Sem.

—And only a man's god would show love for his creation by destroying it.

Noe's face had clouded over no less than the sky.—Take care in tempting God's wrath, woman.

I wanted to say, What can He do that He hasn't done already? But I knew the answer to that: He would lift me up and judge me wanting, cast me aside into the pit of darkness, et cetera, ad infinitum, ad nauseam.

Noe's eyes had disappeared into thickets of wrinkles,

his lips colorless and pursed in their little beard nest. The whole man had gone pinched and pursed, sour as unripe fruit. There was nothing for me to do but turn my back on these zealots and go belowdecks.

That was ten days ago. Noe stayed up top for something like a week as the rain kept falling and the boat slid through the waves and the rain kept falling. Occasionally we'd see a mountaintop struggling to keep head above water but these were few. And the rain kept falling.

I was curious exactly how much rain was coming down, so I took to emptying one particular barrel each time it overflowed. At three cubits tall it fills in half a day, sometimes less. It's quite beyond me to comprehend this kind of rainfall, but there it is. It's not the whole story of course—rain alone cannot account for the depth of the water, now threatening the very tops of the mountains. Are the seas themselves rising?

I wonder what my Phoenician captain would have to say about it, the fellow who predicted the sun's disappearance. I wonder if he'd have an explanation, perhaps illustrated with lemons. A pang cuts me whenever I remember him, or the matriarchs, or my uncles. All gone now. But I can't give in to grief about them—if I start I'll never stop, there are just too many dead, whole peoples, whole civilizations. I hold their memory off, at arm's length, and concentrate instead on measuring rainfall and striving to understand what is happening.

If such a thing can truly be comprehended.

Finally Noe came inside, shaking with fever and half

out of his wits. He collapsed in the family cabin and has been lying there since, shivering under a pile of blankets. Meanwhile Cham and I seem to be the only ones who notice that there's a ship full of animal dung that needs mucking out on a regular basis. Climbing between decks with a bucket of antelope manure on my shoulder isn't my idea of pleasurable, but it keeps me occupied and gets me out on deck from time to time. I wouldn't complain if someone else lent a hand, however.

Sem has taken on prayer duty next to Noe's unconscious body. Good luck to them both. Bera spends most of her time with those two infants. Japheth is uselessly seasick, and Mirn occupies herself playing games with the chickens. To her credit, she feeds the domestic animals too. Cham's mother fusses with the cookfire all day, God bless her. Without her we'd all of us starve.

Once in a while Cham and I pass each other in the corridors down below, and he'll press against me or grab my backside and whisper Got you! and it's almost like it was before. But usually it's not. Cham's a changed man most of the time, preoccupied with leaks and cracks and breaches, taking on himself the whole responsibility for keeping us afloat. And thus alive. I wish there were something I could do, but I don't know enough about shipbuilding. So I haul out the slop and handle some of the fiercer animals he's afraid of, the wolves and crocodiles and lions, who act strangely quiescent through all of this, as if the alienness of the ship's pitch-and-yaw has dulled their predator's instincts. It's all I can do to keep my own instincts under control till the others have gone to sleep in the cabin each night. Then I throw my thigh over Cham's and grope under his tunic for the one solid thing left in this watery world. Beneath me he hammers and rolls but I'm steady as a boat as I ride him and feel a convulsion within me that matches the one going on outside the hull.

They help, these nightly sessions. They help a lot. But they don't do anything to stop the rain, which keeps falling ceaselessly day after day after day. Or to stop the memories of those poor drowned unbelievers on that second morning, or the questions that circle in my mind like vultures: Why me, and not them? Why them, and not me?

There is no answer, of course. There never is.

6
Noe

And the rain fell upon the earth forty days and forty nights.

GENESIS 7:12

It would not be correct to call this sleep. Noe roils in a fever dream of salvation and exile, of God and Hell and transcendent righteousness and greasy sin. Sweat frosts him. He murmurs words, half-words, inchoate pre-lingual sounds. The boat pitches on the swells and he pitches with it. Incoherence kisses his cheek while Delusion mops his brow. They are faithful companions.

—Behold, I am the Lord your God. You shall worship no usurper gods in My stead.

In his watery confusion, his delirious ramblings, Noe stands alone in a stone-walled garden, replete with fountains and walkways of colored gravel. The perfume of unrecognized flowers buffets him. Noe seeks the source of God's voice and sees, on the pathway before him, an ant: smaller than his thumbnail, shiny black, industrious in Its jittery perambulations. Rearing back on four hind legs, the ant cleaves the air with tiny mandibles even as Its voice fills Noe's head.

*—My duty is to command. Whether you act as I instruct
is a function of your own will.*

Something isn't quite right about this scene, this God,
but Noe finds himself unable to focus on exactly what.
He hesitates.

—Do you doubt My power? shrieks the ant.

—Of course not, Lord, Noe gasps.—I serve you
always.

He falls to his knees. In so doing, he inadvertently
crushes the Lord God Yahweh beneath his bony kneecap.

—Lord—?

The insect is a broken smear. Noe reflexively brushes
the wet crust from his body, then arrests his hand.—God
is dead! he wails.—And I have killed Him!

—Truly?

He turns. No longer does he kneel in a garden: now
he stands on the shore of a vast mountain lake. Severe
peaks encircle him like swords. Clean mountain air tickles
his nostrils. Floating on the water, an elegant cygnet faces
him, silky white, black-masked, regal.—*I am the Lord God
Yahweh*, the cygnet honks nasally. —*Look upon Me and banish
your false gods.*

—So I have, Noe answers uneasily. He feels God
should know this of him by now.—So I have long since,
and put myself in Your service evermore.

The Lord God Yahweh swims for a little time back
and forth in the shallows, vigorously wagging His pin
feathers. His neck describes a perfect, graceful arc. Around
Noe, unfamiliar trees burst forth in a hosanna of green
leaves which then curl brownly and fall to the earth.—*If*

you speak true, then show your devotion by performing one last service for Me.

—Anything, says Noe.

—*You do not mean that, I fear*, honks God.—*The spirit is willing but you know the rest.*

—I'll do anything! protests Noe. Sincerity ripples through every fiber of his being: he has never meant anything so truthfully as when he says, Anything at all!

—*Then leave Me alone. Bother Me no more, that is what I want.* The cygnet allows a moment for this to sink in, then with a mighty flap of wings hurls Himself into the air, ponderously, unsteadily, as if preferring by far the watery element to the sky. In moments the bird circles Noe's perplexed solitary figure and wings off, disappearing among the great upthrust sword-points of the mountains.

—Lord! Noe screams, arms upraised.—Do not forsake me!

His own watery echo mocks him: Do not forsake me!

—I have done all You asked, and yet You abandon me! What kind of Creator is that?

—*An unreliable one, perhaps.*

He whirls. Now he stands in high desert, dunes ringing him, piping sun merciless against his head. Before him hunches a lioness whose thick meaty musk cloys his nose and whose eyes burn with dull golden malice.— *Behold the Lord your God. Worship no others in My place, or you will surely perish.*

—I haven't, stutters Noe.—I wouldn't—

—*Give Me one good reason I shouldn't slaughter you where you stand.*

Noe's mind is a puddle.—Lord—?

—*You heard Me.*

Noe finds his voice.—I am innocent of any wrong-doing, Lord. As innocent as a lamb in the field.

—*And we all know what happens to them*, yawns God. Her canines glitter in the desert sun like scimitars. Noe nearly collapses: there is not a blade of grass or inch of shade to be had anywhere in this Pandemonium.—*They are food for wolves. Or men. Either way, they are sacrificed.*

—I have completed your tasks, stammers Noe. He fights the resentment frothing up within him.—Done all you wanted. And now you threaten me? That seems hardly fair.

—*How dare you speak to Me of fair!* the Lord God Yahweh roars in a voice wet with saliva and blood.—*Is the beast in the jungle fair? Is it fair for mankind to claim rule over the creatures of forest and air and sea? When you speak of justice, you really beg for the special treatment you don't deserve.* With this the lioness uncoils her haunches and leaps at Noe's throat.

Noe screams and pummels frantically with his fists, but God has strong jaws.

7
Cham

*For they overflowed exceedingly: and filled all on the face
of the earth: and the ark was carried upon the waters.*

GENESIS 7:18

It's rotten work but the concentration calms me. Being around people too much doesn't suit me, especially here, these people, this much. It's like I'm home again and never left. I know they're family but that doesn't make it better, maybe makes it worse. Is that shocking? Unwashed bodies and staring eyes, all of them saying nothing but asking the same question: Will we die because of you? Of course they put it different. How's she holding up, Cham? or, She taking any water down there? or my favorite: Think she'll make it? Meaning really, Think *we'll* make it? Or will we die, Cham, because you didn't pin a joist properly, or seal the beams in the prow?

So I come down here and inspect. It's a big job, she's a big vessel crammed full of lunatic monsters as ready to tear off my face or kick in my spine as not. It takes a while, swimming through the monkeys that bombard me with shit, ignoring the gazelles while they chuff and stomp and lower their horns at the small of my back. Relaxing work it's not then, oh no, and besides, why am I down here? I'm down here, oil lamp in hand, squinting by its flickering light in order to find a trickle of water between the beams, or a puddle sloshing where there shouldn't be one, or a crack where those rutting huge hippos have slammed their backsides into a weak spot on the bulkhead, any one of which would indicate our quick death in this flailing soup unless I can patch it fast with scrap timber and sludgy tar while the toxic breath of some hateful demon washes over my neck. So no, it's not the sweetest of work, and every so often I'm driven up the ladder again, past the cabin where Abba's sick and Japheth's moaning and the others are ready to ask questions. Past that onto the top deck and into fresh air and wind and rain. After a little time up there, I start to believe that maybe we'll be all right.

We've been afloat now a month. For the last few days the rain has died back from a fierce lashing to a steady light drizzle. Around us is water and plenty of it, but it's all in restless motion, not the feral thrashing of a hurt beast as before, so it's possible to walk around on deck without falling over provided you don't slip on the greasy layer of birdshit. I've never seen so many birds in my life. I reckoned there must be hundreds, until as an experiment I counted those jostling along the stern rail that runs the width of the vessel, fifty cubits across, and found it home to more than two hundred gulls, terns, flycatchers, kingfishers, sandpipers, ducks, finches—and that's about all I can name. Multiply those two hundred by the length of the deck, three hundred cubits, for an idea of the birdlife we're carrying.

I hold out my finger and a tiny little thing lands on

it, no bigger than a grasshopper, feathers shining like green copper and a ludicrously long beak.—Now what the hell are you eating? I ask.

It shifts on my finger but doesn't answer.

A whirl of birds flutters into the air, then settles: Ilya's climbed on deck. She carries a pail of dung to the rail and pours it over. Whose dung was it, I wonder—camel? Anteater? Wildebeest? There's little my wife fears, no animal she won't approach or clean up after, something I never knew about her before this whole wild escapade began. I like it.

—Got you.

—Don't kiss me, she smiles.—I smell like dung.

—So do I, love, I tell her.—Or worse.

It goes on for a time. When I straighten up I say, You're lovely.

She is too, like something chiseled from marble and polished smooth by attentive hands of a gentler make than my own. But lately I've caught her looking wan. Ilya's never given the impression of great heartiness, her strength was always of the bend-but-don't-break variety, and these past weeks she's gotten thin, thinner, till now her cheekbones jut like blades. Which just serves to make her flat-silver eyes even more arresting, but I have to wonder how healthy she's keeping. This business has been hard on us all.

—Look at these birds, she says.

—Yeah. Look at 'em all right.

She gets her distracted look that comes when she's thinking about things.—There should be some way to organize them.

—Organize, I repeat. I scan the birds, there's an awful lot of them.—You mean put them in rows or something?

She smiles tiredly.—Not physically. But in categories, waders and forest dwellers. Insect-eaters and seed-eaters, carnivores and scavengers and so on.

What in Hell is she talking about? I do love my wife more than anything, but when she gets going like this I feel my eyes glaze over and not for the first time I wonder, Where on earth do you come from? What kind of tools gave shape to that mind? Because in my homeland, women aren't—weren't—encouraged to have such ideas, it was all feeding babies and cooking stew and weaving blankets, thanks. And it's not as though men occupied themselves with such pursuits either, what with hunting and farming and so forth. I think to myself, They're different in the north, and this not for the first time either.

As if she can read my face, she hefts her slop bucket and says, I should go. There's plenty left to clean up.

—Do it later.

She wrinkles her nose.—Later there will be more.

—What are the others doing? I ask, more to talk than because I really want to know.

—Oh, the usual. She rolls her eyes.—Cham, I know I'm an outsider here, but it's astonishing how content your family can be to just plant themselves in a tiny room for weeks on end. Even Bera and Mirn.

—Don't I know it, love, it's one reason I had to get out. They're a fatalistic bunch, they could sit there till doomsday if need be.

—It's only been a few weeks, she says with her gray

eyes looking even more washed out than usual.—But I suspect we're a long way from being finished yet. I just hope I don't lose my mind.

—Maybe you'll get used to it.

She grins weakly.—That's what I mean by losing my mind.

It was chance brought us together. She was looking for passage north to get back home after her father died in the wreck, she came to the shipyard by mistake, and I was the only one willing to fight through her wretched accent to figure out what she was asking, and by then it was too late. I was taken by surprise, ambushed in my own territory by the angles of her face and the way they tilted when she asked a question, the way one toe scratched the other ankle. Those ankles were carved by a master all right, and I was good for nothing except grinning like an imbecile and inquiring, Is there anything I can do to help? What I did, naturally, was work as hard as possible to keep her from finding any ship north, meanwhile presenting myself as charming, suave and desirable. Some job that was, and the less said about it the better.

I thought I loved her then. When we married I was dead sure. The wedding was a small thing, a few friends and the necessary authorities, what with her family gone and mine days away and besides, I didn't want Abba wading in and scaring her off with his heavy talk. But I realize now what I didn't know then: I'd no notion what love is. Not the faintest hint. Sure I was ready to jump off a bridge for her, or slap any man who dishonored her. Big deal. I'd lie with her all night and labor the next day to give her what she wanted. So what? That's not love, that's commerce, that's taking care of your property, ensuring that your investment pays a profit, but it's not love by a good many spans. So what is?

Love, strange as it may seem, is what you feel when you watch your wife emptying slop buckets she's collected from some demon-spawned lions and wolves and then tottering away for more, so skinny you can practically see the sun shining through her. And this when there's no sun. Knowing she'll keep doing it, no complaining, because it needs to be done, and knowing you're willing to do the same—no, scratch that, you demand to be allowed to do the same, for her, with anything that keeps you from lightening the burden just an obstacle that's expendable.

When Ilya's next on deck I take the pail from her and dump it myself.—Stay up here awhile, love.

—Later, she smiles, but wearily.

—Now. Right here.

I sweep my arms and clear away enough birds that she can sit with her back to the water barrels and look out over the rail at the waves and clouds, not much of a view I'll grant but the air is clean and the goldfinches and hoopoes are a hell of a lot more palatable than the beasts.

—You can start your organizing right now.

—There's more to do, she reminds me.

I hand her a cup of water.—It'll get done.

Down in the cabin, what do you suppose Sem is doing? Kneeling beside Abba. He's been here without pause since the old man went down, praying and napping and nibbling on whatever Amma's got over the fire, nice work if you can get it. My elder brother, at least, hasn't lost any weight on this trip.

Yet.

I shake him awake and he fixes startled righteous eyes on me.—I'm praying.

—More than one way to do *that*, I tell him, and shove the pail into his hands.—Get down there and clean the stables. We're drowning in shit.

He moves to protest and I yank him to his feet. The trick with Sem is to talk fast so he can't keep up.—Listen. God appreciates work as much as words. Devotion made manifest, get it? Look what He told Abba to do.

Sem stares down at me, wanting to argue but he's too busy treading water to be able to swim. Amma watches us both but doesn't speak. I say, If you want to give glory to Yahweh, do so in a useful manner. Clear the dung out of the damn boat, so Abba has cleaner air to breathe.

Sem twirls the bucket in his hands.—If I stop praying, you think God will understand?

—Oh yes. God understands that you're doing this because you love Him. And Abba.

He nods.

And most of all, I think but don't say, because I love my wife.

8
Noe

His day is simplified to its most basic elements:

1. Breathe.
2. Sleep.
3. Wake, or half-wake, into a foggy semi-delirium in which he chokes out half-intelligible words: Nigh tangles! or possibly Night angles! or maybe even Nightingales! Or perhaps something else entirely— Nice angels?—or nothing.
4. Sip a little water from the cup the wife holds to his chin. Sip a little broth.
5. Chew a piece of carrot or flatbread, swallow it or spit it to dribble down his chin.
6. Have his forehead dabbed with a wet cloth, usually by the wife, sometimes Bera or Mirn.
7. Lapse into moments of hot-eyed lucidity, in which he growls questions about the weather (bad), the boat (stable), the animals (surviving, most of them), land sighted (none), the family (fine, fine, don't

worry about us). Sometimes he gnaws a bit more bread or offers a quick prayer before lapsing again into restless, fevered sleep.

8. Repeat the cycle.

Noe has a conversation with Dinar the peddler, hawk-nosed and sharp-eyed as ever, although dead. A bit of his nose has fallen off. They sit in Noe's old eating room. Noe says, You could have come with us. I told you what would happen. You could have asked to come aboard.

Dinar opens his mouth to answer and water gushes forth, along with seaweed, small fish, the half-digested contents of his lunch. Noe looks away, repulsed. Dinar does not appear to notice: he sits quite close, his knee almost touching Noe's, mouth agape and more water flooding out than could be held by a single stomach. The fluid puddles at Noe's feet, mixing with the room's dirt floor to form a thick slurry of sewage and bile and seawater. Up to his ankles now.

—Let's step outside, says Noe, standing. He tries to lift his feet but finds he cannot. Tries to move his arms but cannot. Panic flutters at the back of his throat: he has somehow become embedded in the sludge that used to be the eating room floor. The water is knee-high, and he is a statue that cannot flee.

Other figures surround him. The naked harlot who mocked him, the others from the shanties that had encroached upon his land. His wife's family, Mirn's mad father. Plus many he doesn't know, or only dimly remembers. The worst are the children, the infants and toddlers who squelch wetly in the mud underfoot, already drowned, reaching above the rising waterline to tap his thighs with tiny balled fists. An old man, sickle-shaped, eyes him with fiery familiar hate, but most of the crowd stare with dull vacant eyes that somehow torture Noe even more than anger would have. All of them vomit water, and much else besides. Outside, huge shadows cross and recross in front of the room's solitary window, and Noe knows the giants are out there too, coughing up lakes of water and acid bile, whole seas of it, oceans. The giants' height will prolong their lives but not save them.

When water reaches his chin, Noe strains his neck to tilt his head ever further back. When it kisses his lips he seals them tight as if to keep the Devil himself at bay. When it brushes his nostrils, Noe begins to gasp and gag involuntarily, to thrash the water with suddenly mobile arms and flexible legs. He smashes down as if beating the vile fluid back by main force. Words rise unbidden in his croaking throat:—Begone! Back! Begone I say! You are all dead, torment me no more!

He wrenches his eyes open and finds a pair of faces floating over his, frowning down like vexed angels. He does not recognize them. They squint at him as if examining a specimen.

—Is he there? asks one.

—I don't know, says the other, older one.—I don't think so.

Noe's eyes jitter with a wordless terror, then close tight, the lids squeezing shut like fists. He is able to shut out the faces of the living, but those of the dead remain vivid and animate in his sight.

9
Bera

The water was fifteen cubits higher than the
mountains which it covered.

GENESIS 7:19

—Leper don't move, says Mirn, pointing at me.

Is this a joke? I couldn't say. My youngest sister-in-law is a mystery to me and I don't expect that to change. Physically a woman (barely), she remains a child in her concerns. Given who she's married to, that might be just as well.

—Leper don't *move*, she repeats, still pointing.

We're all tired. Weeks we've been on this boat already and no end in sight, and if it's not terribly different from keeping indoors through a long cold rainy season, it's not exactly the same either. What with the rocking of the vessel and the endless butting of the goats down the corridor, trying to escape from their pen. (At some point I would have imagined even an animal as stupid as a goat would understand that knocking its head against the wall is pointless. But apparently not.) This cabin is small, especi-ally at night. Smaller even than the old sleeping room we used to share, which was bad enough. Privacy is a luxury that Sem and I have all but given up on, along with silence and fresh fruit.

—Leper don't do anything, Mirn repeats, eyes wide upon me.

All the same, I don't need this. Mirn is at the far end of the cabin by the windows (snakes in her lap this time), Mother by the fire, Father and Japheth stretched along the bulkheads, me with my back to the door.

—Bera, *careful!* Leper.

Which is when I realize her wide brown eyes are looking past me. I crane my head, slowly, suddenly aware of a wet snuffling at my ear. Hanging on the ladder up from the lower decks, rising into the doorway like an unlikely flower, is one of my father's enormous spotted jungle cats.

—Just stay there, says Mirn.

Yes I know. A sudden flinch and it might spring for my neck, pull me down, crush my windpipe. Or if not me, then Mother, squatting with her stolid back to the scene. Or one of the children, or Mirn. (Not so terrible, maybe, but be nice, be nice.) On the other hand if I don't move, it could happen anyway.

We call for help, which arrives in the form of my husband, peering down the hatch from the upper deck, and Cham and Ilya calling up from below. Above the noise of the head-butting goats, the situation is explained and considered. No one quite knows what to do.

—Throw a rope round its neck, Mirn suggests.—Tug it back down below.

Ilya says, Yes, well.

We all ponder but the cat gets bored. Its twitchy nose twitches and its black-irised yellow eyes stare off in every possible direction. Paws are unimaginably huge, and downy. I have to resist reaching out to stroke them. When Father calls out in his sleep the cat (the *leopard*) fixes its stare at him like a carving. But it looks very comfortable, hanging there between decks, and shows no sign of wanting to attack anyone or otherwise moving from its hard-gained position.

—Maybe I should lure it up here, says Sem.

—It'll raise hell with all those birds, says Cham.

—Better the birds than us.

I tell him, You'll put yourself in danger.

—I'll stay out of his way.

I can't countenance the idea, my husband alone on deck with this animal. (I know how fast these cats can run, and Sem is quite a lot slower.)

In the end it is a goat who delivers us. Just as this leopard has managed to climb free of its enclosure, worming through some chink in the woodwork, so too does the persistence of the goats' butting finally bust open a gap through which the largest, most stubborn billy can bully through, staggering out into the corridor on unsteady legs. It announces its liberation with a proud bleat, its terror with a shrill squeal and its sudden annihilation with the silence of the freshly dead.

When the cat is full it is easy enough to lure down. Sem uses a rope not on the leopard but on the remains of the goat, dragging it to the causeway and letting it drop straight to the bottom. The cat, unwilling to lose its breakfast, swiftly follows. Then Ilya coaxes it into its stall where Cham makes a few hasty repairs. When he is finished we all sigh deeply and get back to whatever we have found to amuse ourselves and pass the time.

For me this is the children. The girl is a plucky thing, always ready for a game. If a game can be such a thing as holding out my finger for her to grasp. When she does so her delighted smile, leaf-shaped and ecstatic, seems to lighten the whole dingy cabin. Even those times when I pull my finger away and leave her clutching nothing, her grin is only a little less vibrant.

The boy is an altogether different matter, brooding and glum. (Truly his father's child, except that Sem isn't his father.) Sobering to see in an infant, but there it is. I try my finger-pulling game with him, but when he wins he clings relentlessly and when he loses he squalls. The alternative to letting him win every time is to stop playing. Mother advises me to let him win. Instead I stop playing.

When I offer them my teats they respond ferociously.

My miracle has kept on, day after day. Maybe that's what miracles do, they just keep going. Eventually we forget them but they're still there. When the children are done they roll onto their sides and doze, leaving me to stare out the little square window and imagine all the other miracles that have ended or begun.

At first there were treetops over the water, hardly visible, like ghosts in the rain that didn't fall like ordinary rain does, in drops or for a short time in a pelting spray. This rain fell in white lines in the air, as if laid down by some carpenter's tool, sometimes vertical but more often at a slant. Mountains in the distance heaved pale lavender spires at the clouds trailing down like the muddy bellies of sheep. And everything obscured by those white lines.

The color of water used to be blue, but it has become the gray of the surrounding sea and the crusading white curtains of that storm.

The rain stayed on and the trees drowned and then the foothills. At times we'd pass a bit of colorless floating wreckage, a slab of fencing or an uprooted tree that hadn't been waterlogged yet, or the bloated bodies of cattle fat with gas. Twice I saw tiny human figures clinging to makeshift rafts, waving weakly at us. But we've no means to steer and could do nothing but watch them sweep past.

The water kept rising till even the mountaintops disappeared. I find myself wondering if people tried climbing those mountains to stay above the water, and what they did when the waves drew close. Those last precious cubits above the water would have been the whole world then. People would not have been noble or selfless in any way. They would have been ugly and bitter and mean. Women tossing their children aside, men trampling women. Big men snapping the necks of the weak as they scrambled to reach the very top. People will do anything to save themselves, it is how we have been fashioned.

Anyway, it is done now.

In this cabin there's a lot of furtive whispering about whether our vessel will hold together. For some reason I feel no anxiety. Maybe because of my savage voyage on Ulm's boat, I have faith in this one too. Maybe miracles become habitual. Perhaps having had one (the children delivered to me), I now expect more (the ship to float, the flood to recede, the children to stay healthy). Then again I've lived through things much worse than this stifling cabin and this creaking boat. Or quite possibly I'm just deluding myself.

I do spare a thought for Ulm, though, and his silent crew. Certainly dead now. I hope they did not suffer unduly. (Everyone suffers somewhat.) I hope they are with God now, and content. I am confident this is so.

Though I can't help wondering why this is all happening in the first place. I know what Father's answer would be, and I can imagine my husband's. Neither is especially convincing. I suspect that if I asked everyone on the boat the same question (In ten words or less: Why Has God Done This?), I would get eight different answers in response.

Maybe one of them would help me to fashion my own.

Once the mountains disappear, the rain slackens. It's barely pattering down anymore though the waves remain choppy enough. We're certainly being tossed about, but where we'll end up is anyone's guess.

The children sleep. I squat next to Father and pat his forehead with a rag. Mother sorts lentils for the stew. I ask, How is he?

—Same, she shrugs.

—And Japheth?

She laughs thinly through her nose.—Japheth is fine. He was sick the first week.

This is a surprise. I look at the boy, tucked into the bulkhead.—But he's been sleeping so much.

—Far preferable to emptying dung buckets in the rain.

I return to Father's forehead.—Next you'll be telling me this one's fine too.

Instantly I regret saying it. Her face falls into its usual set of lines.—No, he's not fine. He nearly killed himself. Old fool.

It occurs to me how worried she is, how drawn and yellow her face has become. Anyone else would be weeping with anxiety.—I'm sure he'll recover, I mumble.

She snorts quietly and keeps at it with the vegetables, lentils and chickpeas fuzzy with mold, a few glum herbs.

For all of us, I think, Mother has become our anchor in this flood, inviolate somehow. Food-provider, caretaker. Now I see this journey has been taking itself out on her flesh too. Hair frames her face in limp gray strands and her eyes flicker constantly from side to side. I wonder, Did Father ask her opinion before he started building, or did he just assume she would obey? He does not seem like the kind of husband who often asks his wife's opinion. And now here she is, tending him.

Eager to change the subject I say, The rain's stopped at least. Maybe the flood will recede soon.

Her words are clipped, as by her knife.—Don't know about that.

—At least the boat's holding up.

—Don't know about that either. Girl, listen to me.

She stares at me with a sharpness I'm unused to except from *him*.—You're a mother now, so learn this fast: You can't hope for anything. Just accept what happens. You hope for things, you'll get hurt.

I have no words to answer this.

—The rain's stopped, she goes on.—Has it stopped for good? I don't know. The boat's floating. Will it float tomorrow? I don't know. Will my husband be alive, or my children, or your babies? Will our food run out? I don't know, and I don't hope for things one way or the other.

I'm quite taken aback by her venom.—Good things can happen too, I protest.

She jabs the air with her knife.—So they can, and you'd best appreciate them because there's no knowing when they'll come round again. But treat them as happy surprises is my point.

My hands have fallen into my lap like useless things. Hers charge ahead purposefully, sifting lentils, picking out pebbles. I wait for her to say more but she doesn't, and in fact I'm just as glad. Mother's philosophy is certainly no comfort. But it's one way to survive the day, I think to myself while retreating to my side of the cabin.

It's not until I settle against the windowsill and trace my fingers along the twisty curls of my children's hair that I feel something pushing up from inside of me, like a geyser. It takes me a moment to recognize it: hope. I am quite unprepared for it. Hope swamps my throat, threatens to choke me and spill out onto my children, who are in turn (I recognize this) responsible for my feeling it in the first place. I hope my children will live, and that I will see them grow. I hope their childhoods will be somewhat less miserable than mine was. I hope the waters will fall back and the plants will somehow, impossibly, sprout green in springtime and life will go on as it did before. Except perhaps with less sin, and more approval from God.

Mother would say such fancies are dangerous and foolish. But this is certainly the difference between ourselves and the animals we transport. Does the bull have hope for himself, his offspring, their future? Does the rhino? The toad, the praying mantis? Certainly not. But I don't know how to discuss any of this with Mother, intent on her chickpeas and lentils. So I leave her to her bitterness, though it saddens me to see her so wrung out and hollow. Instead I stare past the window at the endless acres of water, and wonder where we're going. And trail my fingers through my children's hair. And hope we land somewhere safe.

10
Noe

*And the waters prevailed upon the earth a
hundred and fifty days.*

GENESIS 7:24

Noe wakes from deep and genuine sleep.—Thank you
Lord for another day.

The others surround him in moments. The wife
trickles water into his parched mouth.—Not too much.

He recovers quickly. The fever is gone, now it's
merely a question of rest and food. He is skeletally thin.
His first question is, The weather?

—Wet, grimaces Cham.—But the rain's stopped.

Noe nods and everyone waits for the question: How
long did it last? To which they will have to answer, Forty
days, and from which Noe will deduce that his semi-
consciousness lasted five weeks.

But he does not ask. Instead he says, And there is
no land in sight.

—None, confirms Sem.

—Not even mountains?

—None.

He closes his eyes.—Such is the mercy of God.

*   *   *

The morning after his resurrection, Noe is back on deck, surveying the apocalypse. The **torrents** have stopped but the clouds remain. Waves leap and jostle as if animated by all the life they have extinguished. Noe leans against the rail, grasps it with a withered hand. He licks lips and tastes salt.—The animals survive?

—Most of them, answers Ilya.—A few have died, grass-eaters mostly. We fed them to the carnivores.

Cham says, Overall they're holding up. They look fierce enough, but are pretty docile.

—Perhaps the rocking of the boat calms them, suggests Ilya.

Sem frowns.—It sure doesn't calm *me*.

Noe notices that his eldest is biting his fingernails. This is new. For that matter, everyone looks a bit tattered at the seams. No doubt himself included.

—Food? Noe demands.

Ilya answers, They've got enough for now.

He insists on a tour. They take it in stages, Mirn leading him through the upper holds crammed with the restless domestic animals, and then small creatures: lizards and snakes, spiders and insects, groundhogs and meerkats and gerbils and bats and rodents. Some of these cabins have windows open that let in watery light to wash across rooms crawling with squirming, rustling life.

Noe ignores his queasiness and praises Mirn for her conscientious work. He is especially taken by her chrysalis room, its layers of crisscrossing latticework hung from the ceiling of the cabin and supporting thousands of green and brown cocoons.—And these shall all become butterflies?

—The ones that live, Mirn nods.—Usually they would've hatched by now, but these ones seem like they're waiting.

Cham shows him the next level. Mid-size beasts: foxes and deer, monkeys and zebra, wild boar and hyena and thick-backed tortoises. The rooms are darker here, with fewer windows and more teeth on display.—Ship's holding up for now, Cham says, but she's getting tired, no question. I for one wouldn't mind if we made landfall before long.

An awkward silence follows.

Cham points to a pulsing tangle of furry bodies.—Fox pups. Some of the animals have managed to breed, believe it or not.

Noe casts an eye on Bera, on Ilya and Mirn.—A miracle, he says dryly.

The bottom hold is Ilya's realm, shadowed and echoing with surf and wet animal snarls. She takes Noe's hand and holds an unevenly flaring oil lamp.—This can get a bit claustrophobic, she cautions.

—I do not fear.

They tiptoe the length of the corridor, peering into barn-sized cabins. Noe observes, We are walking in water down here.

So they are, two inches at least, rippling back and forth with every lurch of the boat.—Can't be helped, grunts Cham.—The wood sweats.

This part of the ship is black as the Devil's laugh.

From the darkness around them rises a dull effulgence of elephant dung, of rhino shit and wet hippo gas. Sad giraffe eyes peer down from palm-tree necks. Nine-foot tigers raise their heads and survey them with dull-eyed hate. Wolves form ranks and stare them down. Crocodiles appear dead. Camels and buffalo chew cud with torpid ardor while the bears, mercifully, just sleep through it all.

Back on deck Noe is pale. Sem says, Don't worry, Father. We'll make land soon and free them all.

—With a little luck, shrugs Cham.

—It's sure, declares Sem.

—And how did you reach that conclusion?

Sem taps his head.—I've got my reasons.

—Let's hope then, murmurs Bera, ignoring the wife's tight smile.

Noe nods vacantly, as if haunted by what he has seen.—In fact, I think Sem may be right.

Sem is wrong.

The weather turns cold. Damp chill seeps into Noe's joints, his knees and shoulders, twisting him into a contorted sculpture of misery. He wears his pain stoically and waits it out. As if shamed by his father's genuine discomfort, Japheth gives up his malingering and sheepishly begins to help slop out the upper deck with Mirn. The family, long since used to the stuffiness of the cabin, gathers for warmth around the cookstove. The wife keeps the coals stoked and frets about supplies and nobody pays much attention. Noe, sensing that he is the center of his tribe, the core that binds them, calls for stories to pass the time. He is not normally much interested in story-telling, but understands the family's need to remind itself of where they come from and why they are here now.

The others respond with enthusiasm. Cham and Sem offer tales of Japheth's accident-prone childhood: the incident when he tried to sharpen Father's castra-tion knife, or the first time he tried his hand at sheep shearing and nearly disemboweled the poor animal. Japheth retaliates with anecdotes detailing Sem's self-importance (claiming a crow's shitting on his head was a token of God's grace) and Cham's short temper (knocking Dinar the peddler from his horse because he called him clumsy). They talk slowly to make the time pass, adding elaborate descriptions, embroidering con-versations, repeating points of interest or humor. And it works: days go by.

Ilya and Bera contribute their own stories of their animal collecting, while the others shake their heads in wonderment. Ilya tells them of the matriarchs, the council of women who set the laws in her homeland, obeyed even by the men. Noe exchanges raised-eyebrow smiles with each of his sons as if to say *Have you ever heard the like*? Bera treats them to tales of warrior kings and her father's epic, ongoing battles, while Mirn tells them of her girlhood, her young dead mother and broken father and of times before those events: a time she refers to as *when I was happy*. Noe wonders what this choice of words might signify, as do the others. Japheth included. But no one presses to find out.

The wife refuses to talk, claiming she knows no stories, but Noe regales them with tales of how things have changed since his childhood. How the hunters, already dying out in Noe's youth, have faded to dust. How the nomads settled to farm and form communities. How the chipped stone blades of the past have been usurped by costly luxuries of copper and bronze. How he himself had left his family's exhausted lands to seek an unused patch of his own, resettling from time to time as his crops drained the soil.

—It wasn't so easy in those days, Noe likes to say, and says more than once.—It wasn't so easy then.

To which an incredulous Cham invariably demands, And this is?

Over weeks the stories slow to a trickle, then a drip, then dry up completely. Noe keeps it going as long as he can, but eventually he admits defeat. There are no stories left anymore, except the only one that matters, this one they wake up to every morning. The story they are living. But no one wants to tell it yet: nobody knows how the ending will turn out.

Conversation dwindles. There is nothing to discuss except the weather and the animals and they're all sick of thinking about them.

They fall into routines. The daughters ascend to the deck to bathe with pails of seawater in the morning. The sons follow suit at dusk. Filthy clothes are wrung out and hung to dry like banners. This leaves them only slightly less filthy, but everyone is grateful for whatever activity is available. Mirn's new hobby is picking out insect larvae from the rain barrels on deck and feeding them to the birds, who jostle round her like beggars at the bazaar. She claims she does this only with the *extra* larvae, and the rest of the family leave her alone, too enervated to care.

During a moment of lassitude, Japheth invents a game played with chips of wood and a circle of chalk sketched on the floor of the cabin. For some weeks they play obsessively, rolling dice, scrambling to position their markers, inventing new rules. They gamble riches no one's got, finally wagering their only currency.—Three monkeys says I'll pass you this round.

—A water buffalo says you don't.

The wife joins in. Finally even Noe does, casually at first, but soon with a flat-eyed intensity they all recognize. He plays recklessly and loses often. Predictably he is the first to reject the game. The rest follow suit, even Japheth, and the chalk circle grows scuffed and hard to focus on before disappearing entirely.

A new game is invented by Cham. This involves throwing olive pits at the birds on deck, placing bets as to which will flutter into the air the fastest, which will land first and which will stay airborne longest. It is, by common consent, a stupid game. Sem mutters that they are interfering with the signs, but he is ignored. Noe watches for a time, then growls, Careful you don't hurt anything.

—We won't Da, says Japheth.—Just playing is all.

After a time this diversion too is abandoned. Around the ark the water swells and lifts and passes. Noe and his family have all adopted a wide-legged sailor's stance, and all have grown strong in their calves and thighs. Clouds remain, plugging the sky like phlegm, but no more rain falls.

Japheth is the first to grow restless.—Come on, he jabbers to anyone who will listen.—Let's do something. Come on and *do* something!

But there is nothing to do.

—Come on and *do* something.

—Will you just shut up then? snarls Cham.

Noe frowns at this exchange but knows he is powerless to stop it.

There follows a long period of inwardness, whole days spent in the silence of preoccupation or lazy daydreaming. Spouses murmur in quiet half-tone code. Few words are spoken aloud. Bera busies herself with carding and spinning a few stray clumps of wool shorn from the miserable sheep. The wool reeks of urine and worse: she cleans it as best she can, spins it into yarn and weaves narrow lengths of cloth on a handheld loom. Mirn takes turns at the loom in between caring for the animals. Ilya, uninterested in domestic chores, spends long stretches peering at the forest of birds collected on deck. The wife squats and cooks. Noe's sons slouch from one deck to the next, dumping slop buckets, getting into each other's way, growling and snapping and occasionally barking.

At length Japheth and Mirn give up all pretense of

modesty and take to rutting at all hours: in the family cabin, on the upper deck among the birds, even belowdecks in the company of animals. Soon Cham and Ilya, then Sem and Bera follow their example. Noe knows he should put a stop to it but he feels a profound weariness, a physical burden that hampers his twisted body. If they want to rut, let them, he figures. There is little else to do but eat and sleep, muck out the stalls or invent busywork. Rutting seems much the preferable alternative to any of that. And if anyone notices how much the family has grown to resemble the animals in the holds, no mention is made of it.

There are some close calls. One night Ilya's scream rips open the darkness of the family cabin and jolts Noe awake like a kick. Lamps are hastily lit to reveal Cham bleary-eyed in the corner and Ilya mounted on the back of a grinning pink boar. Japheth snatches it round the neck and wrestles it to the next deck down, its heavy, thick body nearly hurling him off the ladder. Sem and Mirn do their best to help. Cham sits up with his hysterically babbling wife, and nobody gets any more sleep that night.

—I thought it was you! I was half asleep but it felt like your leg against me, Oh God—

—It's all right, love, Cham murmurs, like someone soothing a child.—Simple mistake is all.

Another day Noe watches as Bera lifts her son to her bosom and then freezes, her eyes on the floor where her daughter had lain. Before he can speak, Bera's hand shoots out and Noe glimpses what she spied, like a stain against the floorboards: a scorpion, poised and murderous. In moments Bera grabs the creature by the jaws and flings it through a window. Only after it is drowned and dead does she turn to face her father-in-law.

They are silent for a time, watchful. Then Noe says, I wonder if it was one of the last.

—I wonder, Bera replies evenly.

He considers how to proceed. Or if he should proceed at all. This vessel was made to preserve life, yet his daughter-in-law has, perhaps, just destroyed a species to protect her own child.

But when the boy's lips on her nipple squeeze and relax, compress and pull back, Bera's eyes close and Noe knows she doesn't give a damn about the scorpion. He says, I think you would murder any number of them if such were the price for what you feel at this moment.

—Gladly, she tells him. Between them passes a flash of understanding.

And there is the morning when a new, high-pitched yowling floats up from the usual stew of noises belowdecks, a shrieking mix of frustration, pain and fury. Noe finds Japheth in the lowest deck, hoarse from screaming, slumped into Sem. Clutching one hand in the other, blood sticky down his arm.—Mucking the stalls, he gasps.—Bastard lunged at me.

They take him up the ladder to the cabin, where the wife cauterizes the wounds with a sizzling copper pan: the smell of burnt blood chokes the room and Japheth snarls, curses, twists like a snake. Mirn coos to him uselessly and stares at the remains of his crippled hand.

Later he moans out the story. A she-wolf had gone for his throat, he fended it off at the cost of three fingers from his right hand. His thumb and forefinger remain, and perhaps half his palm.

Japheth spends three days in semi-catatonia before heaving himself to the upper deck to howl out at the water. When Noe joins him he repeats over and over:

—It's what I get for pretending to be sick, Da.

And when Mirn hushes him, puts her arms around his stony-hard shoulders, tells him he'll be all right, Japheth asks, What good's a one-handed farmer, then? What's the use of a one-handed farmer?

One day the wife serves eggs and cheese for breakfast, eggs and olives for lunch and eggs alone for dinner. Noe demands, Why no meat?

—Because there is none.

This takes a moment to sink in.—The goats—

—We have six. Kill them now and they're gone forever.

—The jerky?

—Gone.

They all pause to consider this.

The wife says relentlessly, We've chickens enough to keep us in eggs, and flatbread for a time, a good bit of cheese and oil and an olive apiece for a few more weeks. And plenty of water in the barrels, thanks to the rain. But that's it.

The mood turns decidedly gloomy. Sensing the need to salvage the situation, Noe declares, We must be nearly done then. Six months we have been on these waters. I am confident the Lord has not put us to this trial simply to abandon us now.

No one speaks. No one so much as meets his eye, not even Sem.

11
Sem

And the ark rested in the seventh month, the seventh and twentieth day of the month, upon the mountains . . .

GENESIS 8:4

This experience is changing me. I can feel it, can feel myself stepping out from Father's shadow. I have started keeping an eye on things. Someone had to, especially after Father fell ill, and no one else was ready to step up. I'm not complaining. To the eldest falls the duty. But being in charge brings responsibilities, there's no denying it.

I admit to having hopes early on that seem naive now. That the rain would last seven days and then subside. Or seventeen, or twenty-seven . . . I finally resign myself to seven times seven, when lo! it stops after forty days. That confuses me for some time. Then I realize that forty equals five times seven plus five, two less than six times seven, and five plus two is seven again. . . . So it all makes sense.

Then I wonder how long it will take the flood waters to fall back. I never expect this to take longer than the actual storms, but that only shows how ignorant even I can be. Seven days go by, and twenty-seven, and seventy added to seven times seven. Finally I resign myself to spending seven times seventy days on this boat. That is almost a year and a half. If such is God's will, so be it.

Naturally we're all pretty tense. Ilya had been doing just unimaginable things with the water barrels, dumping them in the rain and watching them refill like some kind of simpleton. She has stopped now, thankfully. She's a strange one, you may believe. On top of that the birds on deck were behaving worryingly. I actually saw a pair of chickadees riding astride a flamingo's back! *That* nearly knocked me over, needless to say. When I chased after them they cleared off pretty quick . . . I don't think anyone else noticed.

At least the hawks and falcons have stopped lining up in alternating directions, left-right-left-right. So we can all relax a little. For a time there it was touch and go.

Cham has been insufferable through it all. Bullying me out of praying for Father's health of all things, just to do some menial work that Japheth could have done. Or Mirn for that matter. I'm by no means completely convinced that that Ilya is such a harmless influence on him. Especially after she spoke so disrespectfully to Father . . . But that's another story. I guess. Anyway we have all fallen into the habit of keeping more or less to ourselves, just getting together at mealtimes. Father still interprets the signs from Yahweh, now that he is back on his feet, but sometimes I think I'm the only one listening to him anymore.

Since his accident, Japheth has become, if anything, even more restless and edgy. As I reminded him, at least it wasn't his *left* hand that was injured. But he just looked at me like I was insane.

Sometimes he races up the ladder from the bottom deck all the way to the top as fast as he can, only to slide all the way back down again. He does this many times over. Then he runs the length of the top deck, scattering the birds as he goes, shrieking and cursing. I know we're all at wits' end and he's got his injury besides, but there is a thin distinction between blowing off steam and . . . and acting like a madman. I stay away from him as best I can, let the others deal with him. Just looking at him makes me nervous. Let his poor wife cope.

I have taken to biting my fingernails, a habit I have never been prone to before.

I watch the water and try to understand what it's telling us, but it is hard. The waves flap against each other, wind sprays this way and that. . . . Sometimes it's gray-blue, sometimes gray-green or green-blue or plain gray. None of it seems to matter much. The boat flails along, rolling and diving. It's a test all right, trying to understand this. That much is clear. Sometimes I feel like it's a test I am failing. . . .

But I never quit trying. Better to drop dead right here than to quit.

Bera spends her time with her children. Our children I guess they are. The joke going around is that the boy takes after me but the girl takes after Japheth. So maybe I'm not the real father. Some joke.

*　　*　　*

The whole ship is starting to crumble. There are lizards sunning themselves up on deck with the birds. A drowned rabbit in one of the water barrels. A tortoise in the family cabin one morning, two cubits across at least. How on earth did a tortoise climb the ladder, I would like to know . . .

We try to keep things in their places but it's not easy. There are spiders in every corner, salamanders between the boards, tadpoles in the drinking water. Raccoons have claimed one corner of the chicken stall, while Japheth and Mirn have taken to sleeping in the chrysalis room. What next? Cham and Bera in the elephant stall, I suppose. Mother and Father with the baboons. Everything is starting to break down, the barriers are coming unglued. Any way you look at it, this is not a good sign.

Then it happens. One evening I'm bathing on deck and what do I see but a lump of something jutting out of the water. It's far off so the waves keep rolling in front of it. I fix my eyes on the spot and then what? A little tear appears in the clouds and a finger of yellow-gold sunlight reaches down to illuminate the very spot. Only it obviously isn't sunlight. I just about faint but I guess I don't. The next thing I know the others are beside me, pointing and hollering and carrying on like madmen. Which I guess we are just then. Our cries bring the women on deck and naked as we are, we don't even care.

Just like that the clouds start shredding, sky showing through. I swear I had forgotten what blue looked like, but there it is. I start crying then. We all do.

The ship slides up against something. Shakes along its whole length, then slowly eases to a halt. We stop moving. . . . The birds swirl into the air in a furious multi-colored cloud, swoop around awhile, then resettle.

We stare at each other. I wait for Father to kneel, and when he starts to go down, I drop to the deck myself. My knees crack into the beams. This wakes up the others and they all join us, chastened. But something funny happens. Father seems unable to talk. It is the first time I can remember this happening.

The silence stretches awhile. I realize suddenly how old Father looks, how haggard. His skin is pale and withered, like your hand when you hold it under water a long time. The whites of his eyes have gone yellow. His fingers tremble and he keeps licking his lips as if ready to speak but he never does.

Everyone waits. Frankly this is embarrassing, and besides that it's not the best omen you could hope for. Suddenly I'm a bit impatient with Father.

—All thanks and praises to Yahweh, who . . . who has delivered us from the deluge, I begin.

Father fixes me with a look, but somehow it's not as menacing as it used to be. Not with him trembling like that. He licks his lips again.

I say, Lord, we have striven to uphold your calling. Deliver us now that we might continue with your holy work. Amen.

—Amen, says everybody, except Father.

I look away toward the water, which has dropped enough to show another rocky pile breaking the surface. The first pile of boulders is already twice as large as it was when I spotted it.

—Amen, says Father.

I meet his eye. It is steady now, watching me. He no longer licks his lips or trembles. Instead he holds out his elbow.—Help me up, he commands, and I do.

This next bit is hard to explain. The rain has stopped and the sky is clear, but the water is slow and uneven in receding. It's not like we can throw open the doors and let the animals go tramping out. Where would they go? The boat has settled into a mud slick between a couple of rocky gray outcrops. Before us, and astern, is water. . . . Still we wait.

This is the worst part of all. For two months we sit motionless, resting among mountaintops in the middle of nothing. Without even the sense of floating, the illusion of rolling from one spot to another, the ship feels more like a prison than anything else. Down below, the animals grow restless.

So do we. Japheth foolishly climbs down the aft end of the boat and drops to the ground at the edge of the water. Drops knee-deep into mud and slime. Then thigh-deep as he fights to escape, then chest-high and we all just stand watching him disappear. His arms flail uselessly. He nearly vanishes as we look on, swallowed up not by water but by earth. Were it not for Bera's quick thought to toss him a rope by which we all hauled him out, he'd not be with us this day.

Looking for a sign? There's one.

So that sobers us. We all settle into our routines again. Mother frets constantly about supplies, which are nearly gone, and Ilya reports a similar problem for the animals. We brought hay and so forth but it's nearly used up. I admit, things feel bleak. With the clouds gone, the sun is warming but the air is heavy with damp. Nothing has really dried out. Our skin peels and grows spotty. The Devil's fingerprints indeed! The stars are easy enough to read but the news is mixed. Father says we're nearly at the end, and I don't doubt him aloud, but I guess we're all tired of promises and exhortations and prayers. Yes, even I am tired of praying. . . . That's probably a sin, but might be forgivable, seeing all we have been through already.

Father sends a raven off the boat. I'm not sure this is what I would have done. In fact I am sure it is not. But he is so weak there's no point being critical.

He moves as if possessed, stiff-armed, silent. The birds flutter nervously out of the way. All except the raven, who sits watching with head cocked and a challenging expression. Father bends and scoops it up. The bird is huge, larger than Bera's infants, and so black it is like a shadow in his arms. Whiskers dangle from around its beak and its eyes swim with malice. Myself, I would have chosen another bird.

Father whispers to it. I stand close by and listen.—
Go thou, and find solid ground, and bring us back a sign.

He tosses the raven up, and it swings around in a
wide circle before flapping off to the south. It's a big
stocky bird and we follow its passage a long time, a thick
V-shape lumbering over the waves. It looks none too
comfortable out there, and I can't help wondering how
far it will get.

We wait a week for the raven to come back. It doesn't.

12
Noe

He sent forth also a dove after it, to see if the waters
had now ceased upon the face of the earth.

GENESIS 8:8

Obviously, the raven was a poor choice.

Noe prowls the deck. His thoughts tumble like a
mudslide. Where are You, Lord, that You have forsaken
us here? Are we so distasteful in Your sight that we must
be left to putrefy like rotten fruit?

To exorcise such heretical musings requires physical
effort: Noe closes his eyes, holds his palms to his temples
and squeezes. After a moment he feels the blasphemy pass
from him, out his ears or nose or perhaps some other
orifice. When he opens his eyes the world is again normal.
As normal as it has been lately. Beneath his feet, the deck
lies warm and steady. Noe is almost wistful for the uncertain roll and pitch of the deluge.

His eyes rifle the birds. No point sending another
raven. Then what? Something small, something that will
return in short order if it finds nothing. Something lacking
the stubborn pride that would sooner plunge into the
flood than admit defeat. Something as different from the

burnt-black, rough-voiced raven as it is possible to be. The answer, when he sees it, is obvious.

Cooing gently, the dove floats into the air with the purity of thought.

—Bring us a sign, Noe urges as it flutters off like a bit of cotton, a white speck in cerulean currents.—Come back and show us our ordeal is over.

The dove is gone for a day. Noe monitors the sky the whole time, his neck creaking once again. He dances in place, scanning the cardinal directions. When at last a speck is discernible in the far west, fluttering unsteadily closer, he is jubilant. He raises his hands to Heaven. The bird flits across the waterscape, its flight erratic. Noe's hands slowly lower. The dove collapses onto Noe's shoulder and he brushes it to the deck like an insect. Its tiny chest heaves like a bellows. It bears no signs except those of exhaustion.

Noe's fists are clenched at his hips. For a vicious moment he is ready to wring the horrid thing's neck. The moment passes, but still he does not trust himself to move. The rest of the family, happily, are down below, lost in the torpid semi-paralysis of these past few weeks. That is good. It would not do to be seen like this.

He feels something shift, something drop away from him. Not pride exactly, but not exactly not-pride either. Noe sighs heavily and coughs up phlegm. He is too tired to spit.—Lord, he says, I am nearly beaten. I stand at the pit of despair and look past its edge. I cannot endure much more. My cup is empty.

There is no answer but the laughter of the waves.

* * *

Somehow Japheth is there next to him, hand on his elbow. The whole hand, not the broken one.—Come on, Da. Come below and eat.

Noe hesitates, then follows his youngest down the ladder. As into the very maw of Hell itself, he can't help thinking. Behind him the dove lies nearly dead. A mob of crows and jays, half-starved, tears into it.

13
The wife

While Himself sleeps they sit around talking about him. What's the point? is what I want to shout. Save your breath, all of you. He'll do what he'll do, and all your words won't make a difference.

Fruitless of course; they don't know him like I do.

Sem:—He's been pushing himself too hard. He'll work himself sick again and then collapse.

Bera:—It's the only way he knows how to do anything.

Cham:—There's plenty he hasn't done on this trip.

Ilya:—Let him be. He's an old man.

Japheth:—Anyway, it doesn't make much difference, does it? None of us have any grand ideas either, to get out of this.

Cham:—You could try jumping off the boat again.

Japheth:—Rut yourself.

Mirn:—I think I'm going to throw up.

She goes off and comes back later looking like hell. That Mirn has impressed me these past months; she's tougher than she lets on, and she might be smarter too.

Reminds me of me in fact. No complaining, just getting on with it, though the sheer duration of the voyage seems to have worn her down. I ask her does she want anything, not that we have much of anything left, but she shakes her head no.

The men keep pushing the conversation in tired circles, like oxen wearing furrows into the market road because it's the only path that's familiar.

Sem:—He's still unwell you know. We need to convince him to slow down, and it won't be easy.

Japheth:—He'll slow down when he's dead. The only way he understands life is to live it like he does and no mistake, for better or for worse.

Sem:—Right now it's worse, I guess.

Cham:—Don't know why you're worrying about him so much. He's spent more time on his back than the rest of us put together.

Japheth:—He's gotten this far anyway. Maybe your man knows a thing or two we haven't cottoned on to yet. Ever think of that?

I'm just registering surprise at Japheth's comment, which is the first time I can recall hearing the boy say something even remotely complimentary about his father, when the conversation suffers another abrupt tremor. Or landslide would be more appropriate.

Mirn:—I think I'm going to have a baby.

Pause.

Ilya:—Me too.

Pause.

Bera:—And I.

How's that for a conversation stopper? Three of them in fact. The only thing to top it would be for me to speak up myself, and believe me I'm tempted. But that would be pure mischief on my part. As it is, the looks on these boys' faces suggest they've never heard of babies or paternity or known the logical outcome of all the prodigious rutting they've been getting done with their wives. It's a shock, I'll grant, but please, boys, say something!

And so they do. Japheth is the first, predictably, with his whooping and carrying on like a fool; for a few moments I think he actually forgets about his hand. He's got Mirn rocking in his arms and I swear the poor girl's fit to sick up all over again. Cham's gone all weepy and tender, not at all what one might expect, but that's Cham, always full of surprises. Ilya just shrugs with a what-can-I-tell-you smile. Sem looks more than a little perturbed, or terrified might be a better description, maybe because he's already got two that he's not sure where they came from and what's she doing with another one before we've even made landfall? Bera's face is inscrutable, a mask of some dark clay fired to an expression of mild amusement. She's deep, that one, and gives little away. Sem watches her from the far side of the cabin as if afraid she'll bite.

In the middle of it all, Himself wakes up, smacking his lips and squinting around. I offer some water but he brushes me off and gets to his feet, wobbly but determined. I know the look. Oh how I know the look. We all do; the difference this time is, no one else is paying attention. They've got other things on their minds.

One step at a time, with many a pause and deep

rattling breath, he climbs the ladder and pulls himself onto the deck. It's easy to follow. Outside, the air brushes against my cheek and tangles my hair, which is purely a mess. I've hardly been out here the past six months and it takes a little time to get used to the glare and the birds. My eyes water from the brightness and I darn near step on the critters till I get accustomed to looking down. Then I realize the glare is coming from the deck, which is covered with a layer of birdshit as thick as my finger. Patches of it have dried and peeled up in the sun or been washed off by spray, but as fast as it's gone the birds get to laying down more.

And what do I think when confronted with this sight? I think, What a lot of birdshit.

Once I blink away the glare I see Himself standing a hundred cubits from me, holding something over the railing. I pick my way to him and see he's got a dove in his hands. Against his crusty fingernails and grubby knuckles it practically glows. Not for the first time I wonder, How do some animals stay so clean? While others are plain filthy.

Himself is looking at me.—This will be the third.

I nod.—I heard about the first two. Is it such a good idea?

He says nothing. The poor bird is trembling in his hands. Then I realize it's his hands shaking and the bird with them. It occurs to me to wonder how much longer I might have a husband, and the cruelty of that thought jabs my belly like a broomstick. I think, Hardnosed critter or not, life would be a lot emptier without him. I've a sudden urge to shield him from yet more sacrifice.

This is foolish I know; Himself thrives on sacrifice. It's bread and meat to him, it's air, it's the blood in his marrow. If God ever stops asking for sacrifice, Himself won't know what to do with himself.

But sacrifice is one thing; heartbreak something else again. I say, The first bird disappeared and the second died. Maybe this should wait.

—It can't wait, he answers softly.—We are turning into animals ourselves, on this vessel. It can't go on.

Nothing to say to that, it's true enough.

—Besides, we are to be grandparents, did you not hear?

—I heard.

—Then we must all find our way off this boat.

I admit to feeling a little weepy. I'm not proud of it but there it is. It's not an extravagance I'm prone to. Maybe under the circumstances I can be pardoned; I wouldn't mind getting off this purgatorial boat, myself, and if Himself can find a way to do it, then God knows I'll fall to my aching knees one more time.

The bird scrambles into the air.—Go thou, and bring us a sign, says Himself.

And make it snappy, I think.

We watch it disappear into I couldn't say which direction. It's such a tiny thing and the sky is endless and the sea so huge beneath it. I can't say I'm filled with optimism as to the success of this venture.

We're left alone on deck, the two of us old bones and the birds. The children are still below, talking. About what? Their dreams? The future? What future? Up here all we've got is the past.

Himself looks at me, rumpled. An old old old man, and an old woman.—Well, he says.—We've done something all right, you and I.

And what exactly might that be? is what I don't dare say. As I mentioned, I'm feeling a bit tender. And tired. And about to be a grandmother, three times over no less. For anyone else it would be a time for summing up and looking back over things, but I'm too sleepy. I can't bear to do anything besides curl up someplace warm with a sheepskin over my shoulders. We're nearly out of supplies, I should tell him, but don't. Let someone else worry.

He takes my hand for the first time I can remember. It's such an unexpected action that I stare at his fingers. Maybe he's feeling weepy too, though that would be another first.

His palm is rough and dry, like the belly of a snake. —I almost went back to God these past few weeks, he says. —Forever.

I say nothing. What's to say? I tried to keep my husband alive and maybe I did. Any woman would do the same. But Himself would be the first to remind me that he lived because God wanted him to, not me.

My little brown hand rests in his like some baby creature in the mouth of its mother. Or some wilting prey in the jaws of its master. I close my eyes, too exhausted to make such distinctions anymore.

But the voice grates on like a sandstorm in my ear. He says, You kept me alive, I know that. Even when I was out of my wits I knew it. The demon came for me and you staved him off.

He says, You and Yahweh are all I'll ever have.

He says, No man could ask for a better wife.

I smile a little at that. Probably I should return the compliment, but would I mean it?

He asks, Wife, are you all right?

When I don't answer, he says my name. I open my eyes.—What did you say?

He looks baffled.—I said your name.

—Say it again.

He does. The deck shifts a little underfoot and he grabs my arm. We steady ourselves, two ancient relics in this still-wet newborn world. Some color has come back to his cheeks. His eyes, pale blue like cheap lapis, watch me with a little alarm.

The boat shifts again, settling into mud and silt.

I say, We're nearly out of food, but I should make something for the girls. They need to eat, all of them.

He nods and releases my hand.—What can I do?

It crashes over me then, like surf breaking on a stone: we're alive, and we're getting off the boat soon. Maybe. No, definitely; I'm sure of it. To top it all, my husband remembers I have a name, and even remembers what it is.

I actually laugh out loud. When was the last time *that* happened?

I tell him, You've already done it.

14
Noe

The dove returns that evening. In its beak it bears a twig, new-sprouted, thick with green shoots. Wonderingly, Noe's family passes it from hand to hand.—Olive, says Japheth needlessly. They all recognize it.

In silence they consider what this means. Somewhere the waters have fallen back, the sun has dried and warmed the earth, grasses and trees have sprouted. Somewhere there is forage for their goats, broad empty fields for the animals, flowers blooming, forests replenishing themselves, fresh springs filling sweet lakes thick with spawning fish. In a word, life, taking hold on solid ground. Their need to be a part of it pains them like a wound.

—We'll get there, Noe promises.—Soon.

They believe him now. Their supplies are gone, so what else can they do? For a week they live on dreams and goat's milk and one egg a day. Mirn all but disappears. Ilya turns translucent. Bera shrivels and toughens. The wife collapses inward. The men are bones and beards. Belowdecks, the animals have fallen ominously quiet.

There follows a disturbing night of dreams for them all, dreams of vertigo and restless yawing that fill their stomachs with acid, as if their vessel has come dislodged from the rocks where it landed and moves again on the waves. But not randomly this time: the boat slides forward as if pulled by a tether. It is a beast on a chain, unsure of its footing. Half-blind with its nose chopped off. Unnerving scrapings reverberate against the bottom, sudden wrenchings jostle left and right. After an especially violent crash, the boat slows. Then stops. The dreams end.

At dawn Noe's family wakes as if slapped. Startled into alertness, they eyeball each other and pick at their hair and say: The strangest thing just happened.

PART THREE
SUN

I
Noe

And God blessed Noe and his sons.

GENESIS 9:1

Noe glances at the heavens. A habit he's fallen into, useless now. But hard to break. The sky is empty but for a small band of geese winging south and a few sheaves of benign cirrus.

Noe squints. His eyes are not what they once were, but even from here—he's climbed a small hill this morning, for solitude and meditation—he can make out the family's tents, the grove of fruit trees, the goats in the meadow, the patches of vegetables and wheat, the wandering finger of Japheth's vineyard. Over it all, like a thunderhead come crashing to earth, like a bad memory that refuses to fade, looms the broken hulk of the ark.

Noe figures he'll always be able to see that, no matter how bad his eyes get.

They have been a year in this place.

That first morning they had stood wordless on the empty deck. The birds had already scattered. Noe's family inhaled the virgin landscape spread before them like incense, like an offering. Landscape, not seascape. The vista made them weep: high-shouldered hills framing a valley thick with unfamiliar trees that, even from this distance, could be seen to swell obscenely with fruit. A stream of sweet water burbling through the valley, bisecting lush fields that rolled away to the east in an endless carpet of meadows ripe with flowering grass.

They'd gone onto their knees and prayed thanks. Then Noe said, We've work to do.

The small animals were freed first, dispersing out of sight surprisingly fast. Mirn and Japheth mock-chased them, laughing, into the farthest fields and—lo!—they were gone. Then Mirn returned to her chrysalis room, where she discovered every cocoon open, every chrysalis cracked and shed. The walls around her pulsed. When she threw open the cabin window, a fluttering cascade swarmed into the sunshine: a pillar of flickering orange and black and purple and yellow and aquamarine that rose from the ark like smoke. Like smoke, the column was made of countless tiny individual bits, but these bits contained every color imaginable, and many that were not. Some of the butterflies were larger than her hand. They drifted out over the valley like a promise.

Cham and Bera loosed the fox and monkeys and armadillos, and all the other animals from the middle decks: great serpents as thick around as Cham's thigh, raccoons and sloth and wild boar who grunted and sniffed the air with obscene twitching snouts as if disbelieving what their senses told them.

—Away with you then! shouted Cham as they shuffled or scampered or slithered off.

Bera watched after them wistfully.—I fear we'll never see them again.

—Never is too soon for me, grumbled Cham, clambering atop a flat slab of granite not far from the ship.

Then the swinging doors in the hull were levered back, swollen with seawater and protesting every span of the way. Ilya and Sem led out the last of the cargo. The long-necked, long-bodied or long-snouted creatures from the ark's depths poked their heads out tentatively, blinking and snuffling, scuffing solid ground as if to test its reality. Cham, safe atop his flat-topped boulder, cackled at them.

—Come on, you monstrous freaks! he hollered, standing upright and waving his arms.—You want your freedom, here it is! Now get away from us and for God's sake keep your distance!

The animals bolted, a snarling, trumpeting host. Elephants squelched knee-deep in marshy soil; big cats slunk away like sinners; buffalo and wildebeest lumbered off. Giraffes ambled, zebras trotted, wolves darted. Rhinos stepped carefully, shortsightedly, like old people.

—Adam's rib, muttered Japheth to Bera.—I swear, there's more now than when you brought them.

—Some had babies, said Mirn.

—True, Bera nodded.—But see those gazelles with the twisted horns? I don't remember them at all.

—I certainly didn't bring them, put in Ilya.

Cham squinted sideways at Bera.—There were so

many in those cages, it'd be a wonder if you'd missed none of them.

After a moment, Bera shrugged.—Possibly.

Noe's family watched the hatching in silence. More animals were departing the ark than had entered it, that was clear. The exodus carried on for some time. The wife fingered Mirn and took her away for a while, returning with a basket of apples and grapes and small red triangular berries.—Breakfast for anyone who wants it.

They arranged themselves right there on the boulder. The wife even broke out a little ceramic tub of goat cheese.—Been saving this, she said with a girlish smile that caught the others by surprise.

The sun was halfway up the sky now, the sky itself a flat azure above this luminous green that they could still scarcely believe. The animals had beaten brown trails into it, like threads tying the world together. Still they trickled from the boat that reared against the sky. The family hardly noticed: already the ark had changed from being their entire world to being only a part of it.

Noe's family ate happily, looking around often and exchanging silly grins. The fruit was sweet, the cheese salty and pungent. To drink they had cups of plain river water. It was, by universal consent, the most delicious meal they had ever tasted.

That was a year ago. Since then Bera, Ilya and Mirn have borne Elam, Chanaan and Gomer, bringing the population of their settlement to thirteen. Cham's son Chanaan was the thirteenth. Sem swears this an inauspicious number but refuses to explain why. Anyway it will change soon enough: the women are all pregnant again.

Today Noe has come to this hilltop seeking solitude and, perhaps, communion with the Almighty. He does not hold any great hope for this. The Almighty keeps His own schedule, as Noe knows full well.

—*Noe.*

He nearly stumbles, chastened. The pressure inside his head, though not exactly familiar, is comforting.— Lord?

—*You have done well, and your sons and their wives.*

Noe bows his head.

—*Now there is but one final task.*

Noe quails. His throat constricts and turns pasty. To be honest, he had rather hoped the tasks were done with.— As you command, Lord.

Was this amusement in Yahweh's voice?—*Fear not, Noe. This labor will not be irksome.*

Noe sighs. He can't help it.

—*Hear then My command. Instruct your sons and their wives to go forth into the world, each in a different direction, and multiply, and so refill the land.*

—That's it? asks Noe.

—*That's it*, acknowledges the Lord.

Noe thinks, Knowing my boys, that's a labor they won't carp about. The wives, on the other hand . . .

—*Everything that lives upon the earth*, continues the Lord, snapping Noe's attention back to the present, *shall be delivered unto you and shall be meat for your table. Yet so shall you be for every living thing in all the land.*

Noe isn't sure he's heard right. He squints.—Eh—

—*Whoever slays a man shall himself be slain, for you were made in the image of Me.*

—Certainly, Lord. But I doubt there will be much slaying.

—*You know more than I, Noe?*

He falls silent.

—*Hear then this My promise. Nevermore shall I send forth a flood to destroy the earth.`Never shall I curse mankind and his works. He is prone to evil in his very nature, but I shall not destroy him again.*

Noe gropes for an appropriate response.—Thank you.

—*Behold My sign. And whenever you look upon My sign, remember you My promise.*

Across the sky streaks a rainbow of such intensity it leaves Noe gasping. Spanning from horizon to horizon, it sprays down color like an enormous prism, painting green fields with red, riverbanks with yellow, fruit trees with dazzling indigo. Even Noe's own shadow glows with a crisp blue sheen. He tries to speak but the words cower in his larynx. Then the Lord is gone out of his head anyway, and Noe is alone again.

He takes his time coming down the hill and meets Bera with the goats. The goats have been uncommonly fruitful this year, and two dozen kids scamper among their sires and dams. Bera holds her infant to her breast and watches Noe closely.—Such colors as those I've never seen.

—Hm? Oh yes, says Noe.—Very nice.

—Sem would call that a sign.

—Would he now? Noe makes a point of glancing heavenward, but the rainbow is already fading.—He would know better than I.

Bera raises her eyebrows and says nothing.

The bow is nearly gone when Noe arrives home. It is time for lunch. Conversation is animated as to the significance of the vision. Sem declares, It is an indication of Yahweh's pleasure with us.

—Is it now? says Cham in his needling tone of voice, but he is grinning and poking his son Chanaan's infant belly.

—I think it's saying something else, says Japheth quietly. He sips at the wine he has fermented this past year from the juice of grapes, and makes a face.—Too sour. Anyway, I think it's saying the job's not done yet.

Sem straightens himself in his chair.—And what do you base that on?

—Well it figures doesn't it? You're the expert on signs and omens and portents, Sem. And you've got to admit, they usually happen *before* something terrible takes place, not after.

—Warnings, says Cham.

Japheth gestures with his crippled fingers.—Exactly.

All eyes flicker to Noe, then drop away. He says nothing. The wine they're drinking is Japheth's first vintage, a pale red whose sourness leaves their stomachs uneasy. Japheth has thrown himself into this new project with uncharacteristic energy. Sweetened with honey, the wine is just about palatable to them all except Noe. To Noe the wine is just fine the way it is. He pours himself cup after cup.

The others watch him drink, wondering what it is they're witnessing. A celebration? If so, it is unlike any they've seen before. If Noe is getting drunk, he gives no sign apart from a roseate flush and a slight tremor. He does not grow loud or impetuous or companionable, nor moody, gruff, sullen or hostile. Nor yet maudlin. He remains himself, though perhaps less attentive to the rest of them than usual.

At last he settles back against the floor of the eating tent, their temporary makeshift shelter tacked together from horsehide and bits of the ark's hull. Noe's eyes shut and his mouth falls open and he begins to snore. Gently, as if purring. And although embarrassed at his drunkenness, his infirmity, his old man's lack of concern at how they might be feeling, the others are relieved too that he has gone to sleep. That he has left them, in a way, though he is right there among them. And then they feel ashamed, thinking like that, and wonder at their own meanness.

2
The wife

Sure now and something's eating him. Think he'll tell me about it? Nah. I'm just his wife of fortyodd years, mother of his children, bedmate and helpmeet and all the rest. So we had a little breakthrough on the boat, a little weepy oldperson time. An acknowledgement in a way, of services rendered and long unrewarded. It was sweet and unexpected, and take it when offered is my advice. Now it's gone and believe me, I don't expect a repeat performance any time soon.

Himself is piqued. First glance, everything looks all right. Midsummer fruit swelling in the orchards, goats and sheep prancing in the fields, grain coming along nicely. Children doing well, grandkids ditto, girls all pregnant again, weather beautiful, rainbows in the sky; no blight, no plague, no comets, no rampaging idolaters. No wonder Himself is worried. Too perfect, a cynic might think, and time for the other shoe to drop.

No great odds on guessing it's a vision. A blind man could see as much, which incidentally is what Himself is close to being these days. But it's tough to fathom Yahweh's logic in putting us—and the world—on the chopping block again so soon. I mean enough is enough. Not that it's up to me; we've done flood, but I suppose fire and earthquake are still available, if such is the plan.

I try to get it out of Himself but it's tough going. Woman begone from my sight and all that. But forty years has taught me patience so a few days later I try again.

—Something's troubling you.

—Is that so? he says and strides away. A few more days go by and I get the same result.

Time passes. The moon gets fat and then skinny again. I'm sitting by the river, knocking clothes into the rocks and thinking the flax'll come ready none too soon, we're on the verge of all going naked. Then we'll see about fruitful and multiplying.

Himself appears.—I have need of your counsel, he says as if I haven't been proffering it daily.

I set the clothes aside. When Himself talks it's best to give one's full attention.

—This is onerous indeed, he starts with a weighty shake of the head. I brace myself for the worst. A plague of snakes, maybe, or gout or boils or fire from the sky.

Then he tells me about the boys going off and starting their own little colonies, little nations. And I can't help blurting, That's all it is you're worried about?

He clams up then and I backtrack.

—I mean I thought it was something calamitous, like the end of the world again. This, well, this makes sense if you think about it a little.

His voice is frosty.—Oh?

—Sure. He's emptied the land, now He wants us to go refill it. He's destroyed the nations, so we'll start new ones.

I actually feel a kind of lightness despite Himself's scowling and deep sighs. This river, these trees aren't going to be washed away or burned up. My sons will live, at least for as long as it takes to produce a few children. Not the toughest duty in the world, especially compared to some other things Yahweh might have come up with. Pox and locusts and so forth.

Himself's eyes flicker out across the river.—I had hoped, he begins but doesn't say any more.—I had hoped.

We sit there a time.

At length he says, It will be just us two left behind.

So it will, I think to myself. Maybe that's the nub of it. Is it such a hardship though? I remind him, That's what we started with.

—Yes, but. He spreads his hands.—It won't be easy, the two of us alone.

Maybe not. But it won't be near as tough as it could be, either.—Look at those trees, I grunt with a nod to the apricots.—They're practically keeling over, they're so laden. We'll dry the fruit for winter, same as the peas. Fish run in this stream all year, and they're lazy and fat and slow. Plus the goats and chickens and all. We won't starve.

Himself doesn't seem convinced, so I pick up the washing and get busy with it. While doing so I whisper a quick prayer of my own. Himself doesn't have the monopoly, I shouldn't think.

This is what I say to Yahweh: Thanks for holding off with further calamities. Thanks for giving us poor souls a second chance. And come to think of it, thanks for that rainbow, if it indicates what I think it's supposed to. That the storms are all over, I mean.

He doesn't answer in any fashion I understand. But that's all right; I didn't expect Him to. Anyway, it's enough for me just to offer a few words into the conversation.

3
Noe

*These are the sons of Noe: and from these was all
mankind spread over the whole earth.*

GENESIS 9:19

Six months later the women have all borne their second
children. Daughters this time. It is winter now, and colder
than last year. Fish still run sluggishly in the stream, but
frost sprinkles glittering dust on the ground, and water
left standing at night wears a thin veil of ice in the morning.
The first time Sem encounters this he backs away in terror,
shrieking, The Devil has turned water into stone! Consternation follows, till Ilya explains what has happened. As the
day warms and the ice melts, anxiety evaporates and hilarity
takes its place.

Noe calls a family council in the sleeping tent, as the
eating tent is now too small to accommodate his
burgeoning clan in any comfort.

—In a few weeks you must all leave, he announces
heavily.

Silence greets this declaration, broken only by the
gurgling of infants. At length Cham clears his throat.
—Can you go into a bit more detail, Abba?

—It has been declared, Noe says with a gesture toward the ceiling.

—Ahh.

Noe shifts on his haunches.—The world is an empty place. We have been instructed to fill it. Sem, you and Bera will take your children and travel south. Fill the land with your offspring. Cham, you and Ilya do the same to the east. Japheth, you and Mirn travel north.

—And you, Father?

—Your mother and I will stay here, Noe says. And wither, is what he thinks but leaves unspoken.

A general reshuffling of backsides follows. Noe knows their obedience hangs on a thread: they are comfortable here and had hoped their trials finished. He can count on Sem, but Cham is pouting and Japheth looks confused. It is Japheth who speaks up.—Da, it's the middle of winter. Why travel now, why not wait till spring?

—Planting, growls Cham.

Noe nods.—If you travel now you can sow in time. Travel in spring, arrive in summer, you'll go hungry next winter.

—It'll be hard though, the boy protests.—With the little ones and all.

—So it will.

The atmosphere in the tent is that of a heavy blanket long unused and gone to mold. Even their honey-sweetened wine is unable to lighten it. Finally Ilya says, Our new nations shan't survive long if our children have only one another to marry.

Noe's eyes are like snakes.—A brother wed to a sister

is an abomination in the eyes of the Lord, he growls.
—And their offspring as well.

—I'm not too fond of them either, grunts Cham.

Ilya says, So how—

—You will stay in contact with each other, Noe
instructs.—When the time comes for your sons to marry,
in ten or twelve years, send them to the other families to
find brides. As for your foundlings, Bera, let them choose
who they will.

There are many other questions. Noe answers them
with variations on:

1. Stop complaining.
2. We'll solve that problem when faced with it.
3. God will provide.

Sem and Bera seem generally assured by the last of
these, while Mirn and Japheth shrug in consent to the
first. Ilya and Cham appear markedly unconvinced, especially with the second, but surrender to the understanding
that no further information is forthcoming.

In the subsequent silence, Japheth offers: Anyone for
more wine?

No one is terribly keen but no one says No either.
Japheth passes the jug, and cups are refilled. Noe takes
the trouble to refill his, drain it, then fill it again. This is
observed without comment.

4
Sem

*And drinking of the wine was made drunk, and
was uncovered in his tent.*

GENESIS 9:21

Bera has changed. Seeing her there on the riverbank with
our children, I feel I hardly know her. The toddlers are
asleep at her feet and Elam is pawing in the grass nearby.
The baby girl is nursing. Bera's feet trail in the water with
her skirt hiked up around her thighs. The muscles of her
legs gleam in the sun. She is singing softly, some lilting song
with no words. None I recognize anyway . . . There is much
to her that I don't recognize, even after so many years.

When she sees me she smiles and waves me over.
Not to belabor the point, but this is a change, all this
smiling and singing. Before, she would have waited expres-
sionless for me to come to her. Or not. I take this as an
improvement, you may believe.

We sit for a time. She gestures at Elam, busily tearing out
tufts of grass and inspecting them before letting them
drop.—Checking for omens, Bera laughs.—Just like his
father.

I smile indulgently. I guess I have changed too, and am comfortable with the others' need to jibe at my gifts.
—What do you make of Father's announcement?

Her smile fades.—It's sad. I enjoy it here.

—You think we should stay?

—How can we? Your father says we must go.

—You're not afraid?

—I'm not exactly looking forward to the trip, she smiles wearily.—It will be difficult. But if my last journey was any indication, I don't fear. We'd not be asked to do this, if.

—If what?

—If we weren't going to be watched over.

Which is about as close as Bera has ever come to saying out loud that the Lord will take care of us. Still it is indicative of something, a kind of faith marked by her quiet intensity. I never used to notice this in her, but as I mentioned already, something has affected her this past year. Motherhood, I guess.

Later I say, Have you noticed anything odd about Father recently?

She frowns.—You mean his drinking?

—Yes, I say, relieved.

I won't lie: we have all talked about the wine Father has been putting down. I guess we all just presume he is happy that everything has worked out. Since Japheth's little experiments with fermenting grapes were surprisingly successful, we have tended to wink at Father's indiscretions. Everyone is familiar with his all-or-nothing temperament. But this past week, since informing us we would have to leave, he has been more or less continually inebriated. It's disturbing to say the least. I asked Japheth to hide the wine he has got left, and he agreed till Cham butted in. For reasons understood only to him, he thinks it's funny to see Father in that state. He goes out of his way to keep his cup refilled and nearby. It's infuriating, you may believe. More than once I have been tempted to raise my hand against him. . . .

But I remember the story of Father's ancestors Abel and Cain, and have stayed my wrath. Thus far.

Bera turns to say something. I never hear what it is because at that moment a rough voice hollers out my name.— Speak of the Devil, I blurt.

—What? frowns Bera.

—Nothing.

Cham is jogging toward us, waving his arms and grinning.— Sem, you've got to see this.

I'm on my feet.—What's the problem?

—Not a problem exactly. Or maybe it is.

Cham halts a few yards away, hands on hips and breathing hard. He was always stocky and now he's growing fatter around the middle. This past year of bountiful harvests has settled in his belly. Still as strong as two of me or three of Japheth, but even so a little trot winds him.—You'd best come look in any case.

—Where?

—The tent.

An odd expression on his face, as if he's fighting

laughter even though he protests about the seriousness of the situation. Sometimes my brother is a mystery. . . . I follow him toward the tent, Bera calling behind me Should I come too?

—Probably not, Cham answers. I swear I hear him snicker.

We spy Japheth in the vineyard. Cham calls him over but Japheth is reluctant to give up his work with the grapes. Since our arrival here he has thrown himself into his chores with an energy unlike any I have ever marked in him before. . . . As if trying to do more work with a hand and a half than he ever managed with two. Grudgingly he heeds Cham's entreaties and accompanies us to the tent.

As we walk I check the sky, the trees, the river. Everything looks all right. Certainly no warnings I can see. Even a pair of squirrels peeking out of a tree trunk, cheeks burgeoning, as good a sign as you can hope for.

By the time we arrive I am quite sure Cham is stifling giggles. Japheth catches my eye and I shrug.

—In there, Cham directs us.

The eating tent is empty. We duck to pass into the sleeping tent and nearly trip over Father. He has sprawled crosswise over a pair of sleeping pallets, flat on his back with his arms outstretched. A deep crimson stain discolors the earth near his head. For a horrible moment I take this to be blood until I see the broken cup, the toppled jug. . . . Still this is bad enough. Then there is another thing I see, a moment later.

—Adam's rib, mutters Japheth.

Behind us Cham cackles.—The old so-and-so's gone a bit overboard this time, don't you think?

Father is naked. Scrawny like a featherless hen. His nakedness shames me and I look away, but not before I see his manhood, aroused. Japheth is facing away too. But there are not many places to look in the cramped murk of the tent so we turn back to Cham. He stands framed in the doorway, breathless with laughter.

—Do you see . . . do you see his . . . Oh Yahweh, six hundred years old and still ready for more!

Anger rises in me.—Shut up, Cham.

My brother keeps snorting.

Japheth surprises me by saying, You make yourself small by laughing at him.

Cham wipes his eyes.—He's just an old man.

—Maybe so, I say, but he is your father.

He shrugs.

I feel the betrayal in my own words: *Maybe so.* Meaning, Yes, he is just an old man, but despite that he is your father and so you should pretend to respect him.

Is that what I think?

Japheth slips into the eating tent, where Bera has folded a length of embroidered linen in a neat bundle. He shakes it out.—Give me a hand with this, Sem.

I remember that moment on the boat, when we ran aground and waited for Father's prayers of thanksgiving that never came . . . Instead, I spoke the words and pitied

Father his palsied hands, and helped him to his feet. No, I did not mock him, as Cham snickers now. But was I really feeling anything so different?

—Sem?

I don't know. It's hard to think. Why do people have to change? Why can't they stay the same all the time? Things would be much simpler.

—Sem, come *on*. Hell on earth—

—Adam's rib, giggles Cham.—Look at the two of you.

I seize one corner of the cloth and Japheth the other. Together we walk backwards into the sleeping tent, eyes forward. Not looking upon Father's shame. Cham slinks outside and hocks. Japheth and I cover Father with the linen. Bera has dyed it yellow, a fortuitous color. We pick up the jug and broken pieces of the cup. And stand there.

—What now? asks Japheth eventually.

—Let him rest.

—You'd not shift him around? Put him on the mat the right way?

I consider this.—I don't think so. But it's not good for his head to face sunset, so maybe we should.

We stand a moment. If we move him, we might wake him. Things would become more awkward than they already are.

—Let it be, Japheth says, and I say, All right.

Outside Cham scratches his belly.—Funniest thing I've seen in a donkey's age. Great idea about the wine, Japheth.

Japheth says nothing.

Cham goes on, I hope when they're singing the old man's glorious history, they don't forget to include *this* little episode.

—Just let it go, I say.

—Not on your life, he chuckles.

—There's no reason anyone ever has to know about this.

—That's where you're wrong, brother. There is reason indeed to know: it shows that even the mighty Noe was a fallible wretch, instrument of God or not. A truth that he himself is prone to neglect.

Japheth stares fixedly at some distant point.—Sem. I grunt.

—Do me a favor, would you? Tell your man Cham there that I've nothing to say to him, not now and not ever. Can you do that?

—I'll do it.

—You mind doing it now?

I say the words. Japheth says, Thanks then, and strides off toward the vineyard.

Through all this Cham has been watching with a dead expression of incomprehension. Like something you might get from a smart cow or a dull dog.—What's eating that little twerp, you figure?

I leave him there.

5
Noe

He said: Cursed be Chanaan, a servant of servants shall he be unto his brethren.

GENESIS 9:25

—I may be no more than an old man, Noe rages, but as you are my son I'll not tolerate impudence!

He pauses, considering. A bulbul warbles nearby. Too frantic, Noe decides, and his pounding heart concurs. Try again.

—I am your father—this with a jab of forefinger—and you shall show me respect!

No good either. He sounds petulant, beseeching.

Noe paces the hillside, scuffing up dust devils that twist in the air like wraiths. Maybe:—Is this how you repay your father for delivering you from God's inundation?

A good argument, but Cham will be likely to point out that it was his own handiwork that delivered Noe. It won't do to let him have that.

Noe scrapes together a little pile of pebbles with his sandals, then kicks it. The pebbles fly through the dust devils hanging above the earth, taunting him like the ghosts of his common sense.

This is what he knows. The wife had found him, linen-shrouded and open-mouthed, sprawled across the sleeping mats, and sought an explanation from Cham. This she got. She got others, crucially different, from Japheth and Sem. All the stories were incomplete, but strung together the outline was clear enough. Noe had miscalculated. Cham had rejoiced in the folly and attempted to enlarge upon it. The others had not. When Noe woke, she told him everything. Noe, limp with dishonor, sought his hilltop refuge and appealed to God for guidance.

Thus far God has kept silent. Noe pinches the bridge of his nose and suspects that he has been left to get out of this mess the same way he got into it: alone.

His head throbs like a tambour.

—When you're my age, he snaps at nothingness, at the air, the dust devils hanging in the sky like hallucinatory laundry, *then* you may belittle me.

Another weak argument, and Noe knows it. Youngsters lampoon their elders, it is the nature of things. But Noe's rage is epic, otherworldly. Only with tremendous effort has he managed to keep it in check: his first impulse was to smite his son a mighty blow across the head. But he mustn't give in to fury, satisfying as that might feel. He must temper his anger, explain his wrath, ensure that Cham understands how serious this transgression is. Let it go unpunished and anything might happen. Cham could fall to scorning Yahweh Himself, and feel none the worse. Along that road lay damnation, final and irrevocable.

Noe frowns, breathing deeply. His nose whistles with

the force of his exhalation. Perhaps he has been going about this the wrong way.

Sem is tending the fish traps in the shallow pool. Noe places his hands on his son's head and says, Blessed are you before God.

—Thank you Father, Sem answers, startled.

Barely whispering now, Noe says, Forgive me.

Sem flushes.—It's not for me to do that, Father.

—Do so anyway.

—All right. Sem avoids his father's eyes, bloodshot and watery.—Father, you made a mistake the other day but you have learned from it and you are forgiven.

Noe removes his hands.—Thank you.

Sem blinks rapidly.

—Soon you will all leave me, says Noe.—I have a few reservations about Japheth, and more about Cham. But none about you.

Sem manages a smile through wet eyes.—You have a higher estimation of me than I deserve.

Noe strides off. Behind him in the fish trap, a fat-bellied, silver-sided carp swims in frantic circles, seeking a way out. Sem reaches in deliberately, snatches it by the tail, and tosses it, flopping wildly, onshore.

Noe finds Cham in the ruins of the ark, smashing timbers for firewood. Nearby Japheth does the same. As Noe approaches he observes that although Cham addresses his brother—requesting the crowbar, advising which sections to demolish next—Japheth remains silent.

—Oh for pity's sake! blurts Cham.

Noe clears his throat. They look up.—Oh hi Da.

Cham says nothing. Noe addresses him, full-voiced and deliberate, chin held firm, clasping his staff. With his free hand he gropes at his crotch, cupping his loins.—Cham, this I testify. Cursed shall your son Chanaan be, now and forevermore.

Cham blanches.

—Nothing else than a servant to your brothers his uncles shall he be, Noe goes on, and to the sons of your brothers, his cousins.

—Are you mad? Cham sputters.—Even more than you were already?

To Japheth Noe says, Blessed are you, and blessed are your sons and theirs.

Japheth hangs his head as if it is he who is being chastised.

Cham is nearly incoherent with rage.—You'd all be dead but for me!

—We would be dead but for Yahweh, Noe says sharply.

—To Hell with you then. Next time you've a need, leave me out of it.

Noe fights for calm. Cham has always been difficult, but Noe cannot lose his temper: Cham might not understand the lesson Noe is trying to convey.—Only Yahweh has the power to condemn.

Cham's eyes are startlingly wide.—You'd do well to remember that yourself, he snarls, then stalks from the ruined boat into the heavy sunshine.

Noe sighs. Cham appears to understand nothing.—
Lord, grant me patience, he murmurs.

Behind him Japheth clears his throat.—Da, he says.

Noe does not hear. He walks off in a deep well of
preoccupation. Behind him Japheth hesitates awhile, then
gets back to work, tearing down the ship that has borne
them all to this place.

6

Bera

It looks as though we'll be traveling wet. For some weeks the rain has settled in, no flood this time but a steady chilling drizzle that strips the trees of their browned leaves and settles into my bones. The children seem mercifully oblivious to it, and are as active as ever. But us old folks feel the damp acutely, and I for one fear the notion of riding off to destinations unknown in this misery holds little romance. God will provide, yes, I understand that now. But I wouldn't mind waiting (is this blasphemy?) till He provided somewhat drier weather.

In the meantime there is much to do. We're each to take a pair of oxen and donkeys, horses and cattle (of the type I brought back from my travels, smaller than oxen and more docile, though stupider as well). Six goats and as many lambs and a dozen chickens. Quite the little caravan. Plus the children, of course, four of them now, all toddlers or younger. Sem will have his hands full with the big animals, so keeping the smaller ones healthy (two- and four-footed varieties both) will be my responsibility.

I'm glad we have no fear of bandits, and then I feel quite awful for thinking that way, considering what's happened to the bandits (and everyone else).

The oxen will pull our supplies. Everything we need we'll either carry on the dray or find along the trail, so space is limited to essentials. Some lengths of wool and linen, a small hand loom Sem built, seed grain for planting and some dried fruit, honey, olives, cheese. Little enough to start a new life but after ten months on that boat I've no doubt we'll manage.

As for what awaits us to the south: Ilya is convinced that beyond the mountains we will discover a large expanse of fertile plains, and beyond that the sea. How she knows this is quite beyond me, although she is prone to wandering off for half-days at a time, so maybe a steep hill some-place has afforded her some clue. She claims that the rain is blowing up from the south, and this indicates the pres-ence of water some distance away. Moreover, she says that much rain has already fallen before it reaches us, so there should be many lakes and rivers where we are going. Although I hope she is correct, her thinking quite baffles me so I maintain my silence.

The twins are starting to talk now. They've been making sounds for a while and some of them pop out as words. They call me Mama and Sem Papa. The first time he heard that he turned his face away but I could see he was very moved. My husband does not show a great deal of emotion, which is something I like about him, being the same way myself. But he has a large heart. It will be interesting to watch him grow old.

The other day the boy began chirping, Yahweh! Yahweh! Yahweh! I looked into the sleeping tent to find the child on his knees, pointing at Noe. The old boy looked half-asleep and fully mortified and I can't blame him.

—Grandfather, I corrected, lifting the boy.—That's Grandfather, not Yahweh, silly child.

—Yahweh! Yowwee! Yoyoyo!

My father-in-law blinked sleepily above his tangle of beard.

—Hush now, I said.

I carried the child into the other tent, ostensibly to feed him but really because I was about to snap a rib laughing and I didn't want Father to see.

Today I'm weaving bolts of cloth to take along. Ilya spins listlessly on a hand spindle while Mirn cards. I've done more than my share of weaving already but I don't mind. I enjoy the feel of the threads under my fingertips, love to see the shuttle pass and the fabric grow, strand by strand, taking form and texture as I look on. Mirn on the other hand is an indifferent weaver, easily distracted (the grain of her fabric is erratic, with gaps like missing teeth) and Ilya is quite hopeless. It's painful to watch her labor at something she so palpably hates. I feel sorry for her children, who will probably spend much of their youth unclothed.

The rain lightens but does not cease entirely. It is of a piece with the cooler temperatures and longer nights, which together pass for winter in this land. I say as much.

Ilya replies, In my homeland, winter nights barely end. The sun is hardly above the horizon long enough to be seen before it sets again.

Mirn stops her carding and stares at her with eyes like a frog.—What do people do then? I mean, what *did* they do?

—Little enough, she shrugs.—Drank endlessly. Told stories that never seemed to end about warriors slaying one another.

I say nothing, but our men tell similar stories. Told.

Ilya goes on, For months on end the ground is covered with snow, a white powder made of frozen water. It is difficult to get about at that time.

I try to imagine the picture, green land gone white, but I can't. What would it look like under the full moon? Mirn's mouth hangs open. I imagine Ilya has lots of fun telling us gullible southerners all manner of dross, and giggling to herself when our eyes pop.

Well, we've all got a story of our own to tell now, the story to end all stories. (That nearly did exactly that, in fact.)

I'll miss Ilya and her tales. I'll miss Cham too, for all his gruffness. He's another who hides his softness with a frowning exterior. Sem is still cross with him for something he won't explain in any detail, but Cham's been nothing but kind to me. With the children he's a revelation. They adore him.

Mirn and Japheth now, I don't know. She's a happy-go-lucky thing and I don't know why that should grate, but it does. Maybe looking at her, I'm reminded what my own condition was at her age. I had already been through more misery than she'll ever know, and somehow her presence makes that all the more palpable. Is that unfair?

Certainly. Would I want the same for her? Certainly not. But I can't help wishing there was a little more substance rattling around that empty head.

Japheth may be in the process of growing up. Those months on the sea have affected him, as they did all of us (except, alas, Mirn). And of course his accident. It's quite admirable how he has pushed himself since. Still, it's a mystery which Japheth we'll meet each morning: the loud-mouthed child who laughs too much at all the wrong things, or this new hybrid, quieter and soberer. He's far more industrious than before, I'll grant him that.

And of course Mother and Father. They've certainly been a presence in my life. After all, Father bought me and gave me to Sem, and that debt can never be repaid. (I'd likely be long dead if not for his intercession, after a short wretched life whoring in some slum.) Altogether he's treated me as a better father than my own sire did. Mother is a low-key presence next to him, cowed some would say but I know that grandiosity isn't her style. Fatalism suits her better. I wonder what she thinks of all of us going out on our own. It would be a difficult thing to face without hope.

Oh Hell. It's tough enough to face the future with hope, and plenty of it.

And I've finally asked the question. Over the past year I've managed to be alone with each of the family for a few moments and put forth that which has troubled me since the beginning: *Why did God do it?*

Father:—Because He wishes to cleanse the world of sin and punish the unbelievers.

Mother:—Because He can.

Sem:—Because He wants to encourage us to do better.

Cham:—Because He's got no respect for His own creation.

Ilya:—Because, like most males, He loves destruction for its own sake.

Japheth, in a low monotone while staring at the twisted bird-claw remains of his right hand:—Because He's the boss and don't you forget it.

Mirn:—Because He wants to see what we'll do.

None of these answers is satisfactory, but my own (because there is no limit to the suffering He makes available to us, for reasons only He understands) is no more so. So after everything, I'm left where I was at the beginning.

After supper Sem pulls me aside and says, Good news. I spent the day traveling south, along the route we must follow. The others did the same.

—And?

—The first day or so we simply follow the river. The way will be easy.

—That's nice to hear, I agree.—Something easy for once.

—After the first day, though, the river angles west.

—Oh?

He licks his lips.—Then we will be walking directly into the mountains, at least for a time. But there is no reason to expect they will go on for any great distance, and on the other side we may well find land as fertile as here. Or better.

—All right.

—I'm sure we'll manage, Bera.

I think of Ulm and his rickety barge.—So am I. But I'm confused as to why this news should please me.

—It has to do with the others. Mirn and Japheth travel north and they can just follow the river for days, as far as we can tell. Maybe weeks. There are no mountains to the north.

I giggle. I can't help myself. I poke a finger into his chest and say, The good news, Sem.

—Hear me out. To the east where Cham and Ilya go, the land appears flat, a plain more or less. It looks dry, but even so . . .

I'm smiling to show him I don't mean it when I say, You're quite mad, you know that?

He frowns.—Why?

—I must be the only woman alive whose husband thinks it is *good luck* to get the hardest task assigned. That's what you think, right? We're blessed the most because we're being asked to do the most?

—That's not what I meant at all. It's good news that the others will have it so easy.

—And we'll suffer. And suffering is good.

—It's not that suffering is good, he sulks.—Though it is true that—that—

—Being asked to do a great deal gives you the chance to show that you're willing to do a great deal.

He gazes at me for a time while he unties that knot. It would be possible to draw Sem's portrait using only straight lines and still achieve a reasonable likeness. This is even truer when he is frowning in confusion, which happens quite often.—Yes, he says finally.—I guess so. And you think that's foolish.

—I do not.

He is pouting.—You think you have a simpleton husband who enjoys pain.

I kiss him then and there, right on the pout. (No one sees, we're alone by the stream.) It occurs to me to wonder where the children are, but I let it pass and let the kiss linger.

That quiets him all right.

—I think I have a husband who is concerned with doing the right thing, and unconcerned with what it costs him.

—When you say it like that it sounds so simple-minded.

Which is in fact the opposite of what I believe, but I don't bother explaining this. I just kiss him again.

7
Noe

Noe has sworn off wine. He tells Japheth: Before leaving, tear out the vineyards. Bring with you whatever cuttings you want, I'll not need them.

He expects an argument, but his youngest has been obedient ever since the inundation.—Sure Da. I'll take care of it.

Noe watches Japheth heft the ax awkwardly, his left hand doing the muscle work, the shattered right guiding the handle. The tool swings in an uncertain arc that pounds as much as slices timbers into ragged firewood. The pitch-soaked boards burn smoky but hot, and this winter has seen them demolish one-third of the ark. Its holed bulk hovers behind their farmstead like decayed carrion, like a reminder of trouble gone by.

—Japheth, Noe says.

The ax drops, the timber cracks but doesn't split. Japheth grunts; his breathing is labored. He swings again and this time the wood shatters. The pieces are tossed onto a growing pile.—Yeah, Da?

Noe hesitates. There are many things he would like to say but his tongue is unused to the shape of the words. Words like, You've done well I'm proud of you, or, I am impressed by how this adversity has steeled your resolve, or even, I'll miss you and Mirn. With his children, Noe's vocabulary has always been that of action, of deeds good and evil and consequences to match. This is what he knows, what he's comfortable with.

Japheth is squinting at him.—Yeah Da?

Noe points to the wood.—You've quite a pile already.

Japheth nods.—I need the practice now that God's made me a cripple.

Noe winces.

—Besides, I wanted to leave a bit for you and Ma.

—Yes, you'll be leaving soon. He hesitates.—Best make sure Mirn takes along everything she needs.

—I'm sure the others have told her, Japheth shrugs, but then adds after a moment, But yeah, I'll check.

A pause. Then:—Da, there's something I'd like to mention.

—Go ahead.

Now it's the boy's turn to hesitate.—It's about Cham.

Noe says nothing.

—What Cham did was awful and deserves to be punished. But, ah.

He falls silent.

—But what? prompts Noe with iron in his voice.

Japheth knocks the ax butt against his calf.—But Chanaan shouldn't be made to pay. It's not right. He's just a babe and's got nothing to do with it.

Noe contemplates the sky with his lips pressed tight. There are a few clouds today, high up, white as angels. Noe remembers the angels from the deluge. He's not seen them since.

—It's not right Da.

Noe says, This is what you wanted to tell me?

Japheth lifts the ax again.—Yeah it is.

Noe watches as his youngest hurls the blade against the wood. Anger bubbles up and threatens to engulf him but he bites it back till his jaws ache. Carefully he says, Thank you for the wood, son.

Japheth goes on chopping long after Noe leaves him. The pile he's got already is nearly as tall as he is.

8
Cham

Some kind of gratitude, isn't it?

The day we're all to go off it stops raining and the sun chases away the clouds, of course that's taken as a sign from the Lord that this is an auspicious occasion, blessings will tumble down from Heaven to delight our progeny and all the rest of it. I'm happy enough not to be hiking in the rain but I'm not prepared to say the clouds drying up is an omen from the Creator of all things to myself personally, the way Abba and Sem are all too eager to do. But that's my family for you, a sense of their own cosmic insignificance is one thing they most definitely do *not* have.

Anyway I'm happy enough to be going, the way these past few weeks have been. I won't deny it hurts but there are some things I'm ready to leave behind, for instance the dirty looks I've been getting from them all, you'd think I was the one getting tanked and waving my rod in everyone's face. And the things he said about Chanaan being their servant, those words echo in my head and I start shaking all over, I lie awake at night thinking about that till I'm ready to jump up with an adze in my hand and do violence to something. Let them try to make my son into their servant. Let them just try.

You could do some serious damage with an adze. I hate thinking like this, it's just as well we're leaving.

We're all gathered in the clearing in back of the tents, each of us with our baggage and beasts facing where we're headed: Japheth and Mirn to the north, Sem and Bera south, me and Ilya east. Count on us to be given the worst route, away from the fresh water and easy fishing of the river and into uncharted emptiness, no thought about what we'll subsist on or the fact that what grassland we've spied from here seems markedly empty of trees for such basics as campfires. Pointless bringing this up, it's no accident we're being taught a lesson but naturally there would be great protests if I suggested as much. Rut him then. I'm equal to any task he faces me with, as I've shown already.

Amma's there looking miserable. I give her a hug and she clings to me without a sound, she's never rejected me, God bless her. I think of the first time I left home years ago and how hard it was for her then, this time is worse by far.

Abba clears his throat and I know he's up for making a speech whether we're interested or no.

—This is a great day, he starts.—This is the day which the Lord has appointed for us to complete the work He began.

If that was just the beginning, I think to myself, I'd hate to see the end.

There is a pause. Maybe Abba's wondering what to say next. Amma rests her head on my chest and I listen to the rustle of jays in the willows along the river and despite myself I know that there are things about this place I'll miss.

Abba says, God creates and God destroys. Two years ago He destroyed. Now, using us as His agents, He will create again.

Amma straightens up and pats my chest, watching me with a tight smile. She's not dropped a tear and do I expect her to? Don't count on it, she's a tough one, my Amma.

—There is something I want you to remember as you make your way forth. All of you, Abba says with a significant glance in my direction.—Work as industriously as you can, but remember, God reigns over everything.

Don't you think He's made that abundantly clear? is what I want to shout, but Sem is staring with his mouth open as if this is all fresh bread, and Japheth who used to be an entertaining little wiseass not so long ago now stands with his hands behind his back and eyes on the ground like some pillar. The boy's been taking himself just a touch too seriously ever since his beard passed from fuzz to whiskers, which come to think of it took place some time ago. Sorry about your hand, kid, but sulking won't bring it back.

—God reigns over everything, Abba repeats in case we missed it the first time.—Surrender yourselves to Him, even as I have, and you shall find the same contentment.

Is it a wonder I don't laugh out loud? Yes it is but I'm exercising truly remarkable restraint. Forgive me Abba but of the many qualities you've demonstrated in my lifetime, contentment has been notably lacking.

In any case he's done. Stiff hugs all around then, for Sem and Japheth and even myself, am I supposed to feel flattered? Grateful? Then Sem shaking my hand mumbling Good luck Cham, and Japheth turning his back on me as if I'm unclean, suit yourself, boy. Amma all fragile-looking among the grandchildren and Ilya, Mirn and Bera in some sort of weepy-giggling huddle. At length we all take our leave and it's none too soon for me.

I look over my shoulder a lot that first morning as the grassland we enter rises a bit from the river valley, not enough to be a real climb, but enough so the elevation gives a view of the farm falling away. The river is like a winding silver sash bordered with green, with our little patches of cultivation hugging its edge. The tents and animal pens look like toys, and even the remains of the boat, leaning heavily like a ruin, soon grow tiny. Amma and Abba shrink to doll-size and then ant-size, then I don't see them at all. From time to time I catch a view of Sem or Japheth or more properly their animals, a straggly line of them hugging the riverbank. Seeing them like that, creeping north and south with our own trail beaten into the prairie behind us like a plumb line in chalk, ready to disappear, brings home to me just how alone Ilya and I are going to be.

Ah, but that's all right.

She seems fine with it too. I catch her eye as we make our way this morning, ask How you holding up? and generally keep an eye on her. She's resilient in her way but she's also one to keep her complaints to herself, which is not a problem except that sometimes she overdoes it. At times I think our daughter's birth was more difficult than she let on, and that was only a few months ago.

We make pretty good progress considering the babes and animals. Ilya leads the donkeys up front, with the infant on her back and Chanaan riding alongside, goats and sheep trailing along on a ragged line that they constantly tangle and trip over, snatching mouthfuls of grass at every opportunity. I'm at the rear with the dray and the oxen, stubborn beasts ordinarily but happy enough given this easy walking to plod along so far. We'll set no speed records but neither do we stop overmuch.

Every so often Ilya calls a halt to untangle the goats and collect a few stones from the trail, somehow she always finds them, and builds a little cairn. Waist-high seems to be her preference, but she settles for less if the rocks aren't at hand. She's no mason, the towers wobble and tilt with corners jutting in all directions, though I suppose short of an earthquake they'll endure well enough. Never figured my wife to have an artistic side though.

—What's that for? I ask.

—To find our way back.

I grunt. To be honest I'd never given much thought to going back.

—Or to help someone find us, she adds.—Like Bera or Mirn, or their children when they come to get married.

—You girls work this out among yourselves?

—It was Mirn's idea, she smiles dazzlingly, and I think, When will the earth run out of wonders?

By midday we're well into the plains, with the valley we've left barely a green stripe on the horizon. The sky's patchy with clouds and though it's a pleasant enough afternoon I know the evening will be damp and cold, even with sheepskins to wrap up in, so I've a notion to put one edge of the dray up on stones as a shelter, angled up to keep the rain off. Ilya smiles at me when I mention this.

—You're such a clever man.

—Right you are.

—What are you looking at, clever man?

To be honest I'm looking at my infant daughter hanging on my wife's left teat and Chanaan working on the right, but it wouldn't do to say as much though I'm not sure what's holding me back. A year or two ago I'd have said it. Maybe I'm turning into an old respectable patriarch, what a pity that would be. Just like my father.

—I'm looking at our children. They seem sturdy enough, no?

—They take after their abba, she nods. Adding with a smile, Praise Yahweh.

—Yeah. Praise Yahweh.

Though if you ask me, Yahweh hasn't done a great deal to earn my praises or anyone else's, unless you consider the world's biggest demolition job to be something to sing about. He's a master craftsman I'll grant, but unlike most such He's short on respect for the things He builds and a touch too eager to reduce them to dust. I for one wouldn't shed too many tears if Yahweh just kept His distance from here on out, we might all live longer. That's probably a terrible sinful damnable hellfire-deserving thing to say but if my father's taught me anything over the years, it's that that's the kind of man I am.

We sit like that for a time, me and my family, then pack up and move along. At sunset the sky is clear enough but I go ahead and try my dray-as-shelter experiment anyway and a good thing too, as in the middle of the night we're both awakened by a soft drizzling patter that soaks into the prairie grass and keeps straight on through till morning.

9
Noe

—Thank you Lord for another day, he recites every morning before falling silent. The health to enjoy it? A labor to perform? He has no labor other than the mundane task of keeping his body alive, a body that pains him in ways previously unimaginable. Only a hypocrite would be grateful for that kind of health.

Noe broods. This is not how he'd pictured his old age, alone with the wife like a pair of lepers. He had expected to be the patriarch of an ever-expanding clan, a universe with himself at its core. Now the children were gone, grandchildren out of sight, God uncommunicative. This last bothers him most of all perhaps.

For a time he throws himself into daily chores, telling himself he'd missed the peace and quiet. He tends the goats and chickens and two remaining cows. He shears the sheep with the aid of the one good knife they've not given the children. He busts the clods in the wheat field and nurses along lentil seedlings and mustard. The wife observes all this from the doorway of the tent, meanwhile weaving linen and churning butter and setting yogurt and salting down the occasional butchered goat.

Spring wheels slowly past. The days grow warm.

The wife watches closely as Noe splits a cord of unneeded firewood to add to Japheth's stack. When he starts clearing brush for another field, she comes outside to tell him, There's just the two of us you know.

—Chickpeas have to go in somewhere.

—The patch behind the sleeping tent was enough when we were thirteen.

He doesn't answer. His body heaves up and down, up and down like a pecking hen as he bends to grasp the stringy bushes and heave them from the earth.

She says, I know you want to keep busy.

—Let me be.

—But there's no running away from it is there.

He faces her, red-eyed and manic.—What are you babbling about?

—We're alone now, she says. Her own eyes flicker like candles.—We've all we need. There's nothing to do but sit and rest and enjoy the calm.

—Pfft.

—Lord knows you've earned it.

—We earn what the Lord sees fit to give.

She tucks threads of gray behind her ear.—If you want something to do, you can set the cheese and churn butter.

—Those are your jobs.

—If you could do them one time I'd be grateful.

There is an unfamiliar timbre in her voice. Noe notes

that the wife looks a little washed out. And why not? She'd been working hard too.—Show me how, he says.

She leads him back to the tent and instructs him in making butter and cheese and yogurt. Noe learns how to salt down fish and debone a chicken, how to press olives for oil and filter the smut from honey. All this takes many days, in between his other chores.

The wife teaches him how to pound flour, how to make dumplings and noodles and thick stew. Fruit will not be in for weeks but she assures him there is no talent to drying apricots and peas. Curing olives is a little trickier.

—In the meantime, she says as her nimble fingers pluck a wad of raw wool, I'll show you how to card and spin and weave.

—Wool or linen?

—Wool first.

Noe throws himself into these tasks with typical single-mindedness. His weaving is far worse than his cooking but the wife is patient and Noe is obscurely grateful for the diversion. Once more he begins each day by thanking God for the labors to come.

Only once does he ask her, half-jokingly, What will you do when you've made me as good a wife as yourself?

—Sleep, she answers without a trace of irony. The dullness of her voice snakes through his belly like venom. He realizes her gray pallor has become permanent.—Sleep for a long long time.

10

Ilya

*Out of that land came forth Assur, and built Ninive,
and the streets of the city, and Chale.*

GENESIS 10:11

I feel I'm forever starting over. When my mother died I
went to my uncle, then he grew ill and my father took me
with him on his voyages, though the family warned it was
no life for a fourteen-year-old girl. That existence was another
adjustment, but surprisingly I thrived until his wreck, and
then followed my marriage to Cham and the years in that
seaside town, then our life with Noe and the flood and afterward. And now this. I don't wish to sound ungrateful: people
who don't start over, die. I understand that, and I appreciate
the chances I've had. But as I said to Cham last night,
Enough is enough. I don't think I could start all over one
more time.

He nodded.—I agree with you, love.

—If I have anything to say about it, my children will
spend their whole lives in this place.

Today he's out with the oxen, clearing another field
for next spring's planting. I'm fortunate—my husband is
industrious and sensible, not to mention strong-backed.

It's midsummer now and the wheat is coming along, a small patch but it should do for us. Next year when Chanaan is on solid food and Leya is older, we'll need more. We've been lucky with the land, a nice wedge situated between two adjoining rivers with good drainage and plenty of pasture. Not many fruit trees, and I'm hesitant to sample the unfamiliar types that are here, but Cham was so taken by the location that we settled. In any case I was in no mood to argue after three months of trekking.

The journey wasn't as bad as it could have been. The first month especially was relatively easy—as easy as walking six leagues a day could be with two infants and a string of domesticated animals in train, over unknown territory with limited supplies. But at least the terrain was flat. The grasslands quickly gave way to rolling high-dune desert broken only by a winding creek that we clung to as if to faith itself. The sun burnt down like the evil eye and we took to traveling from dusk to sunrise, easy enough with the smell of water to follow. At length the creek bent southeast and widened into a stream as a range of low stony mountains came into view. Low, that is, for anyone not looking to cross them. Cham sniffed out the easiest passes he could, but still the ground was barren and broken. Hiking those hillsides left me with cramps that still twinge in my thighs on chilly mornings. That, combined with the backache that lingers on from Leya's birth, left me near-paralyzed on more cold mornings than I care to remember.

Along the way I left plenty of stone markers, practically every hundred paces. We changed direction constantly.

Those stones provided another mystery, as if I needed

one. Dull gray granite and flint gave way, as we climbed higher into the mountains, to a sandy red stone layered with quartz or some other dull-white mineral. Cliffs reared above us for hundreds of cubits, their faces layered with countless stripes no thicker than a finger—innumerable hands placed one on another.

—What do you make of this? I asked Cham, but got only a grunt in response. His attention was taken with the livestock, who found this trail difficult going.

The real surprise was at the top of the pass, after we had ascended more or less continually—with many switchbacks and rockfalls—for three weeks. The stream dwindled to a trickle. We'd stopped for lunch, and I was squatting on the rough sandy ground, nursing the children, hoping the water wouldn't dry up entirely. My back throbbed and my eyes roved aimlessly over the earth between my feet, and what should I notice but seashells.—Well now.

Cham was unimpressed, but his nonchalance masked unease.—Many are the wonders of Yahweh, he muttered. —God made the mountains, why shouldn't he put seashells here too?

—Granted. But why bother?

I reached to pick up a shell—there were thousands of them now that I looked, fragments of cowries mostly and some scallops, their ridges unmistakable—but the children hampered me.—Why would God scatter cowries on a mountaintop, unless they lived on land at some point?

He snorted.—That's outlandish. You might as well say this mountain used to be the bottom of the ocean. Which a couple years ago, it was.

True enough, but this explanation isn't satisfying. It seems unlikely that so many creatures would have been carried this high, even by waves as powerful as the flood's. Again, many of the shells were pitted and worn, the color bleached and faded, the animals long dead before they arrived here—not living creatures swept along and then dying after the water fell back.

Another mystery. I sighed—another explanation, I was certain, waiting only to be chanced upon. Like the meaning of the constellations, or the secret of how birds fly. Did Yahweh pepper the world with conundrums such as these for His own amusement, I wondered, or did He do it as a challenge to us?

We took the better part of a month getting through those mountains, and I won't soon forget the feeling in my belly when we mounted the last ridge and looked down across the vast flood plain, opened before us like a luxurious green carpet.

Cham twinkled at me.—Your new home, Ilya.

I dabbed my eyes.—It's lovely. Let's get down there.

—Got you, he said.

We still needed three days to descend the mountains after one of the oxen twisted a foreleg and slowed to a hobble. Then we were on the plains and Cham wasn't content until we'd made it to the riverside, but when he got there he decided its shallow banks were prone to flooding and he wanted to push on to higher ground. This took another week, and then he spotted the other river and wanted to see if they met anywhere and ten days on we saw that they did, the land bulging between them as if squeezed between two hands.—This is it, he said and I agreed.

It's lovely land, a thick triangle bracketed by the rivers, with soil that crumbles black between my fingers and a sheen of prairie grass shimmering as far as the distant mountains. Our livestock is growing fat on the grazing, and Cham says that sowing is as easy as rolling downhill. We feared we'd put off planting till too late, but summer here is long and it stays mild even at night. So we've been lucky that way, or blessed. Blessed I suppose, but it's hard to think of blessings given all that has happened.

Two months we've been here already and Cham's got the fields in good shape. The soil is lush and easy to plow. The house is no more than animal skins stretched between cedar trees, but Cham promises to construct something more permanent this fall. The rivers are thick with silt and have clay banks that could be cut and baked into bricks to keep the winter out. Silty or not, the river is swarming with fat-bellied, orange-gilled fish that kept us alive our first month here.

Every day brings a surprise. We'd been here a week when I awoke not to Cham's usual morning flurry, but his body heavy and warm against mine. The youngest was whining and Chanaan was tugging my arm for breakfast. There was no fire—Cham usually does that—and our little skin shelter seemed joyless enough that dawn, slick with dew and knifed through by cold little breezes.

I poked him.—You sick?

—Mmnf?

—Why aren't you up?

He raised his eyes to mine.—It's the Sabbath, love. Day of rest.

I was so startled I couldn't speak. He'd observed the Sabbath before we'd left but I thought it Noe's influence. Cham hadn't worried much about the Lord's day since his shipbuilding years at Za, and I told him as much.

He rubbed his eyes.—Building the ark didn't leave much time for relaxing. And in the flood, we had things to do every day.

—And here we don't?

—Course we do. But all in its time, love.

Yes, well. He'd barely cleared and sowed the wheat and vegetable patches, but so be it. We still needed water and a fire and something hot to eat. By the time I finished doing this he was up, playing with the children on the dirt floor of the shelter. I admit it was sweet to see the three of them like that, and for a time I joined them.

After lunch I said, I'm going for a walk. Watch the children?

—Sure.

The afternoon was lovely. I walked in the direction we'd come, long grass kissing my knees, poppies all around in a sea of red. There was no trace of the path we'd trampled a week earlier.

I walked a mile, climbed a little rise and looked over my shoulder to our skin tent, barely visible in the distance, hung among the cedars. Beyond lay the Y-shape of the rivers' confluence. At the top of the rise I came upon the little cairn I'd built on the way here. I'd been tired then, and the cairn was a pitiful knee-high excuse for a marker.

Now I took the time to dig out a few good-sized stones, the biggest of them a full cubit across, and built them into a proper little tower. I didn't stop till it was waist-high and sturdy enough to withstand all but the most relentless storm. On top I placed a direction marker, a heavy wedge-shaped slab of quartz pointing directly at our settlement. Then I moved on.

The next cairn was stacked perhaps a mile further along. I'd done a more substantial job with this one but I rebuilt it anyway.

That afternoon I refurbished only those two towers before returning home. But as the weeks pass and the wheat grows taller, it becomes my regular Sabbath-afternoon activity. Before long I'm taking the donkey and covering a greater distance; eventually the horse takes me even further. Without staying away from home for days or weeks I'll never be able to reach more than a fraction of the cairns, and in years to come, I expect I'll do just that. The work is soothing. I'm not afraid to admit the cairns are an umbilicus that stretches back to the only family I have. The idea of losing that family, of their losing and forgetting us, fills me with an anxiety that no night on the ark ever matched.

Perhaps I'll look for those cowries again someday, once I get back in the mountains. Collect a few and try to comprehend how they got there. Compare them with the few I've carried ever since my years at sea with my father. Perhaps they are different in some way that can explain the mystery in the mountains. And perhaps—there are many perhapses, I know—perhaps they will explain a thing or two about Yahweh as well.

Like how He could have done what He did.

The matriarchs of my homeland are gone now, and the goddesses they worshipped are gone with them. Oda is dead too—no great loss. But some of the goddesses had more to recommend them than Oda, busy devouring her enemies and bathing in their blood. Some of the other holy matrons were gentle and compassionate. Good mothers, the kind I'm trying to be. They didn't drink blood. For that matter, they didn't drown the world and everything living in it, either.

It seems to me that Yahweh has a thing or two to answer for. But I'm the first to admit, there's a lot I don't understand. So I'll get back to the mountains, one day, maybe years from now, and collect those shells. Some of them were even embedded in stone, odder still. I'll study them and try to understand what they're doing there, and perhaps through understanding Yahweh's creation, I can understand Yahweh. At least a little. Perhaps by understanding Him, I'll better understand His motivation for destroying so much of the beauty He had wrought.

It's the least I can do, I suppose. Give Him the benefit of the doubt, try to understand before passing judgment.

More perhapses. Most likely I'll just get old and shriveled and bitter like Cham's mother. Then I'll die. And then, if my father-in-law is correct, I may get the chance to ask a few questions after all.

Cham comprehends none of this I know. When I go out riding, he just thinks I need time to myself. How ironic that is, his believing that I wish to be alone more than we already are. But he never asks what I do on my Sabbath afternoons, and I don't volunteer. It's clear he is not much interested in maintaining family ties, at least for now, and theological debate doesn't hold much allure for him either. He's got enough on his mind as it is—the crops, the livestock, his nascent building projects. He certainly earns his day of rest. I think he dreams away most of the Sabbath, and I don't blame him one bit.

11
Noe

The illness is unlike any he has witnessed before. The wife's malady is marked not by fever, aches or delirium, nor yet by sweats, insomnia, vomiting or tremors. Her eyes flare from her pallid face while weakness leaves her too enervated to rise from bed. Apart from this she claims no discomfort.

Nor does she lack energy to issue instructions.—That cold cellar needs tending.

—I'll do it, replies Noe dutifully.

—Dig it out and line it with stones so the crops don't go moldy. I told Japheth last summer but the boy never listens.

This is the fourth time she has told him, possibly the fifth.—That's a fine idea, he says.—I'll take care of it.

Her gaze wanders up the walls like an insect.—You'll need a good heavy blanket before winter. Don't forget. We gave all our best woolens to the children.

Noe bows his head.

—Where are the goats? she blurts suddenly.—No

one's watching the goats, you haven't let them run off have you?

—They're in the meadow, he assures her. But when she leans back her fingers still worry the hem of her linen.

Noe dotes. He devises brothy soups as savory as he can manage, and feeds her himself. Her twiglike fingers rest on his forearm as he holds the spoon to her mouth. He has sheared the sheep and stuffed the wool into a pouch of linen on which she lies, relieving her tired joints. She smiled at him teasingly the first time he laid her down, and seemed about to speak, but dropped into heavy sleep before the words escaped.

While she dozes, which is much of the time, Noe tends the chores that need his attention. This takes no great effort. The farm has been set up to sustain a large family but now supports just two people and soon, Noe knows, only one. Gradually he does less and less, allowing ripe fruit to fall uncollected and leaving three-fourths of the wheat to revert to wildflowers. Meanwhile lentils spread like weeds, and clever hens roost beneath their thick cover, having learned that Noe rarely seeks out more than a handful of eggs. It is rare that he butchers a goat or wrings a chicken's neck. As if in response to his neglect, the farm around him surges with life.

Noe spends much of his time in prayer, or at least in directing his thoughts toward the Infinite, which is what he has always taken prayer to be. Now he is not so sure. God's silence is complete. As a younger man, Noe would have raged and railed at his wife's illness and cursed God's indif-ference, then apologized and beseeched His intercession while silently boiling against the injustice of it all. But Noe is no longer a young man. He is not two or three hundred anymore, and he has lived through more than any other man ever has or will. Through painful experience, he has learned that the net result of raging and railing and cursing and beseeching and boiling is: nothing. The Lord does what He wants, when He wants it. At the moment, for reasons no human consciousness can fathom, He wants Noe's wife to die.

But slowly. Noe can see as much and it fills him with sadness like water in a well. Threatening to overflow. The wife is being kept alive long enough to instruct Noe on how to keep himself alive, hence the lessons in cooking and weaving and the rest. Even his eyesight has improved over these past weeks. Clearly God means for Noe to go on living at least for a time. Noe being the man he is, he must wonder to what purpose.

Standing amid the apricots, Noe bows his head.— Lord, send a sign of Your intentions, he says aloud.—Show me You are not displeased with me, and that this is not punishment.

Punishment is what Noe fears this is.

A squirrel skips between trees, tail held high, and scurries lightly up a trunk to lose itself among pale silver-green leaves. If there is meaning in this, Noe cannot read it.

His voice quivers. It is little more than a whisper.— Lord, I have done all you asked. All that any man could, and more than many men would even try. If you've a task for me, show me what I must do. If not, if not—here his voice breaks, the whisper nearly choking off—please spare my wife.

Yahweh is silent.

—She has been faithful to You too, in her way. Look on her fondly when You call her back.

Yahweh is silent.

Noe stops talking as well. He makes his way to the tents and sits on a stone and looks about him. Sun cascades cheerily across fields and meadows, vegetables and fruit trees, river fat with fish, sheep fat with wool, goats fat with goat. This is his own little nation, a kingdom of one with himself as ruler and subject both. His paradise, his garden, his Eden. Soon he will be alone in it.

The thought makes him gag.

12
Japheth

We'll have a Hell of a story for the grandkids.

I feel a little bit bad turning my back on Cham like that but the rutter had it coming. The way he treated your man was monstrous. Sure he's a bit much at times and no mistake but the man's six hundred years old and that's got to count for something. Cham well and truly deserved whatever he had coming, although I do think your man overdid it a bit bringing the curse on Chanaan's head. I'm glad I spoke up about it and I'm even gladder we've left it all miles behind us now and weeks in the past.

I never complain though Mirn and I are given the absolutely worst route to follow, due north into cold country where, if Ilya's tales are any guide, winter lasts ten months out of twelve and the ground is full of stones. We follow the river the whole way with those Godforsaken fat fish. Two weeks out I'm so sick of fish I can't bear the thought of another one. Then Mirn goes, Ready for some fish? and there's no choice, we've little else to eat except some cold provisions and we've had it with them too. So

I snatch a couple fat-and-stupids from a shallow edge—
I've gotten pretty good at using my left hand for that—
and Mirn guts them and fries them in a little oil and salt.
It'll keep us alive for now but the whole while I'm chewing
I've got my eyes on the sheep, thinking, Before long this
will be you my friends and no mistake.

Mirn never gripes and you've got to love that. Mind
you, I don't think she's exercising any great control: I think
she truly isn't bothered eating the same thing day in day
out, fried fish for dinner cold fish for breakfast. She's always
going, We're blessed with such abundance here, and all
this. I just shut it out. I've thought more than once that
my wife's got an empty head and a lovely behind and this
journey proves my point.

Anyway I don't mind her chattering on while we eat.
It helps take my mind off that rutter Cham and the hollow
look in your man's eyes the morning we left. Like he'd
been kicked in the apricots or something. I'm not putting
all the blame for that on Cham but it's clear that leaving
on such a sour note was tough on your man. My brother
could've at least apologized, not that it would do any good
but it would've been something.

Oh look, Mirn goes, those big orange butterflies.

She hasn't lost her taste for little creepies and bugs
and whatnot. Often as not when it's time to move in the
morning she'll be on her knees in front of some locust
or ladybug or tadpole. She's forever picking up stones
to look under them, then stacking them up with a pecu-
liar intensity into big piles near as tall as she is. It's cute
to see her taken with such unimportant nonsense but

it's draining too. All the serious work falls onto my shoulders.

Ah well. She's a good ma for the kids and no mistake, I'd not deny that.

Three weeks after our departure, the river winds down into a nice bit of valley, grasslands on either side rising in a series of flowery hillocks that grow gently steeper. It's pretty countryside and full of Mirn's butterfly friends, not to mention all manner of woodpeckers and warblers that wake me up every morning with their Godforsaken racket. We're tempted to drop our bags and settle then and there, but I've a notion we've not yet gone as far as we ought. After all, your man told us to go and settle new nations and this is still the same river where he and Ma are, a bit further north but the same valley. It's tempting to stay but we push on.

Some days later the river is joined by another from the northwest, wider but still shallow enough to cross. There's fish here too but of a different kind and all I can think is, Something else to eat. So I go, Hey Mirn should we go this way? and she goes, Okay. And that's about how much thought we put into the decision.

For a while then I really wonder if I've been stupid. The land starts out okay but goes dry after two weeks and starts to rise, turning stonier and harder with every step. This is good for walking but rotten for planting. We're by now approaching a month and a half on our feet and thinking it would be pleasant to settle, but not here on this dry light-brown sand, with hills before us and the same behind for a good long stretch. Another week we press on, following the river as it rises and winds through rocky outcrops thick with thorny scrub and tough grass and not much more. The odd yellowjacket buzzes my ears. Those river fish save our lives then and no mistake. There's not a drop of rain to be had in this whole locality, which gives me pause concerning farming in the region. There always seem to be clouds in the distance before us but it's like chasing a mirage. I seriously consider turning around each morning but, remembering your man's experience with the boat, leave things up to Yahweh and get on with it.

Mirn is bothered by none of this. Ignorance can be a great blessing sometimes.

Another week and we can make out a great ridge rising ahead of us, unusually flat, like a tabletop. The hills we climb through ripple away from it like waves on a lake. Waterfalls hang off in white fingers, and the river we're following seems fed by one of them. It's still three-four days' walking with all the animals, but if we can get up there and scout around, we'll have an idea what's ahead of us and maybe plan something.

We stop to eat: hard biscuits, olives, dried fruit. Mirn goes, Look at the rabbit.

Adam's rib, thinks I.—Mirn, listen. See that ridge up there?

—Mm-hm. Plateau actually.

—What?

—It's too flat to be a ridge.

—Hush up a minute. I've been thinking, this land around here is awful. Too hilly to farm and the soil's useless anyway.

—One leads to the other, she goes. As if she knows the first thing about it.—When it's hilly the water washes all the good soil off the top.

God in Heaven, it can be frustrating trying to talk to her.—Mirn, pay attention. We get to the top there, we'll take a look around. If we like what we see up ahead, we push on. Otherwise it's time to backtrack to where the rivers meet up and try our luck the other way. It's a long walk but I don't know what else to do. I'm half-crippled and can't make a go of it with soil like this.

I admit to being discouraged, sick of this walking and anxious about my hand. It won't be easy, being the crippled farmer, it's not something I look forward to. The past couple years I've taught myself, true enough, learned to hold tools differently and gotten my left hand pretty steady. But it's not something you're ever truly comfortable with, losing a hand. Someone who says it is, is someone who's never done it.

Mirn however seems unperturbed, staring around herself as usual. I follow her look and see some big orange-and-black birds, orioles she calls them, tramping through the scraggly bushes.

—Have you listened to a word I've said?

She faces me then with her round smiley face and brown eyes that taper a bit into points. She's beautiful, I have to say, and I'm ready to roll her over then and there and all is forgiven, but she drives me half mad when she goes, We'll like it fine up there I think.

—How can you say that? You've not seen it.

—Well, there's orioles and bees and rabbits and—

—Adam's rib, Mirn, don't be such a rutting child.

Right away I'm sorry I said it because her face crumples like a piece of cloth in your hand and she starts crying.—Come on then, I go.—Come on, I didn't mean it. I'm stupid, hm?

She nods.—It's just—It's just—

—I'm sure it'll be lovely there, I say. Though I can't help adding, Little rough without a drop of rain though.

She wipes her eyes.—Of course there's rain. There's a river, right? And waterfalls. They're coming from either a spring or a lake, probably a lake because of all those clouds. The plateau catches all the water dumped on that side of the range. That's why it's so dry on this side.

Listen to her rattle on. I put my arms round her and squeeze her and go, It's all right, I'm not mad with you. Just tired.

She leaves muddy streaks when she wipes her face.—Orioles eat fruit so there must be fruit trees around there. And the rabbits eat something too. The bees need flowers. I don't see any flowers here, do you? Somewhere there's a meadow with dirt good enough to grow things.

She points ahead of us.—There probably.

I follow her finger and have to admit, it makes a pretty picture, but I know I just want to believe it because I'm tired.—Your da teach you all this?

She half-laughs, half-sobs.—Daddy was in no state to teach anybody anything.

Isn't this a puzzle, thinks I.—So who showed you? Or do you just make it all up?

—Oh Japheth, she goes, and I swear it's like listening

to my own ma.—You don't need people to show you things. Just *look*.

If that doesn't beat all. Obviously she's still upset, so I lean her into me and give her a squeeze the way she likes. One hand, one claw.—I'm no good at looking. That'll be your job from now on.

She doesn't answer. I tell her, What I'll do is I'll plow the fields and tend the animals and all that, and build you a nice house up there out of timber, if there is any. Or mud otherwise, or even stone. I'm not afraid of hard work anymore. I used to be but now I sort of like to see how much I can do. I'm a changed man now, really.

She smiles at that and goes, I know it.

—But your job is to look at stuff and figure things out and tell me what to do, okay? And teach the kids. When they get older they can help with the heavy work, but you'll have to be the brains of the operation. Because Yahweh knows I don't have many.

She giggles.

—We're agreed then? I ask her.—You're willing?

—All right, she goes, and burrows into me.

Poor thing. I think she really believes it.

13
Noe

And Noe lived after the flood three hundred and fifty years.

GENESIS 9:29

He buries her in the soft soil of the field he cleared for chickpeas but never planted. The earth parts as easily as water. He lowers her shroud-wrapped body into the hole and shovels in loose dirt, tamps it with his own gnarled feet, and shovels in more. By the time he is done the midday autumn sun burns coldly on his shoulders, and his threadbare tunic is sopping. Not until he has rinsed himself in the river and dried his stubbornly vital body does he allow himself the luxury of sitting at his dead wife's feet, and weeping.

It is quickly done. Noe contains about as many tears as a stone, and they do not flow easily or for long.

Afterward he gazes about him. The field has been reclaimed by scarlet poppies, long-stemmed and black-centered, and though they are gone by now, he knows that in spring they will encroach to wreath his wife's grave. Another season or two and they will have obscured it entirely and that, he decides, is fitting. Some of the pagans used to mark their dead with carvings and towers and proud monuments of all kinds, but this is a vanity that Noe wants no part of.

He clears his throat and murmurs, Thank you Lord for another day.

A little later he adds, Though the labor You have given me, I would have preferred to put off for a time.

The Lord's silence is universal.

Noe imagines the future stretching before him, unrolling like a river or an endless bolt of cloth. He pictures the years of his life piling on, decades or possibly centuries alone in this place. Going through the daily rounds of tilling and harvesting, of calving sheep and weaving garments. The thought of it fills him with a kind of dread, sticky and black like tar. Thought of his progeny is the only thing that can chase this despair away, his grand-children and theirs, coming to pay him respects or even live with him for a time. Desperation fills him.—Lord, he whispers, don't let my family forsake me. Send them back on occasion, to remember an old man who once did Your bidding.

Yahweh says nothing, and the knob in Noe's stomach remains.

He hears a snuffling. He turns his head to find himself staring into the quizzical russet face of a fox, white-eared and alert, poised twenty cubits away. The fox stares at Noe gazing at him, then trots off. Noe knows he should rouse himself, scare the fox away lest it steal a half-grown goat or a few chickens, but doesn't have the heart. Let it stay. Perhaps it will become a companion to him, snoozing outside his doorway at night. Noe well understands the pathos in this.

The sun ducks behind a cloud and everything dulls a bit. Noe wipes his eyes on a sleeve. Moisture has collected in the corners, like dew.

He remembers their last conversation. She had been lively, even chatty. Noe had sat next to her and wondered if she were at last recovering. Something moved her to observe, You're preoccupied lately. Is it another vision then?

He shook his head.—No.

—You sure?

—Oh yes. He permitted himself a small smile.—The opposite, more like.

She frowned.—What's the opposite of a vision? A blindness?

—Something like that.

She cackled, not with meanness but warmth.—Yahweh's not been in communication, I take it.

He shook his head.

—So it goes, husband.

And after a little while she added: Toughest test of all maybe.

He sighed.

—Makes that flood look like nothing, doesn't it? Just a story to scare children.

—I don't follow you, he admitted.

—Oh husband. The test doesn't end when the flood does. It's only the start.

She leaned against the pillow he'd made her, eyes

glittering but flesh spectral.—Without Yahweh whispering in your ear you're no more nor less than anybody else. No special assurance that you're blessed or that God gives a rat's ass what happens to you.

Noe stared at the dirt floor. Such thoughts had crossed his mind, in slightly more refined terms.

The wife said, Bury me in a field of wildflowers, would you?

—All right, nodded Noe, but he was preoccupied by the words she had spoken earlier.

After a time the wife smiled and closed her eyes. To Noe she said, Now you're just like the rest of us.

They sat for a while without speaking. Noe stared at his toes, knobby and yellow-nailed. At length he said, Do you think I'll find my way then? The way you have all somehow managed?

He thought he heard her whisper, God knows.

—Eh?

There was no answer. He looked up. The wife was dead.

14
Mirn

When we reached the top of the ridge and looked over it was just like *Heaven* lying there waiting for us.

—See? I said, but J. just stood with his hands opening and closing.

The ridge dropped down a little ways and then flattened out in a plateau just like I'd said it would. There was a big lake bang in the middle and flat land all around with little clusters of trees. Wildflowers wound through them like a rainbow that had fallen down. Piles of cube-shaped rocks cropped up here and there, heavy for sure but good for building walls: cover them with mud and they'd be warm all winter. Looking down I could picture it all the way it would be in a year.

Ducks swam in the lake and honeybees buzzed the lilacs.

—Adam's rib, J. kept saying. It's the only thing he knows to say when he's surprised.—Adam's rib.

The cow went moo. Poor thing was two-thirds starved after those dirty dry mountains. I said, Let the animals go.

—They might run away.
I pointed.—Would you run away from *that*?
I was right. I usually am.

Now it's a year later and it's almost like I pictured that first day. Besides Gomer our oldest and Nasra our baby girl we've got twin boys, Magog and Madai. I've got my hands full looking after them plus the animals *and* the cooking, but J. does his share and more with tending the fields and his building projects. It's amazing what he's able to do even with his hand twisted up like a crab's claw. He likes to say, There's work to be done and I'm the one to do it. He looks so serious when he talks like that, and I can't wait for these kids to get old enough to *help* their father.

He also likes to say, I'm a changed man now, and it's true, he is. Except that he hasn't changed toward *me*. He still thinks I'm silly and simple and I guess he always will. It's okay though. I don't mind if I'm always his little Mirn. Sometimes the hardest things for people to see are the things that are right in *front* of them.

Last fall J. finished our permanent house, a single room for both sleeping and eating. It has a wood roof with turf on it and a window over the cookfire. J. had trouble with all that lifting till I showed him how to use a lever to shift the heavy rocks. Even so he had to build a kind of stone staircase outside the walls, hauling the stones up one step at a time in order to finish the top part. Later he admitted it was the hardest thing he'd ever done, and the thing he was proudest of. It's a low room anyhow, barely tall enough for him to stand up straight. But I was right: layered over with river mud and sand, it was snug the whole winter, which was long and boring. For three months the ground was covered with *snow*, as Ilya calls it, white and pretty to look at but burning cold to touch. The ground underneath froze as hard as desert pavement. Even the *lake* froze over. We stayed inside most of the time, looking after the kids and hoping for the best. It was almost like being on the boat again.

This spring, on top of everything else, J.'s busy building shelters for the animals. He's already finished a little henhouse made of stones that I helped clear out of the fields. Last winter a few of the goats and sheep froze in the cold, until J. and I moved them inside with us at night. The chickens stayed inside too, even the cows. We sent them out in the morning, but it still felt like we were living in a barn. And I thought J. made noises in his sleep! I'll never complain again. J. says next winter he wants them to all have shelters of their own.

Fortunately the spring's been mild and we've made up for most of the animals we lost, and now the cow's with calf. That'll be something. I've never birthed a calf before, but J. says it's nothing hard, especially after helping me with the twins. Says the cow will do most of the work, just like I did, ha-ha. We'll see. Sometimes I think J. tells me things so I don't worry even though he's not sure what's going on either.

Last fall all the ducks left the lake, stretching their wings like they were waving goodbye before zooming away low over the water. I was sad to see them go but now I know the cold would've killed them. Sometimes I wonder how they could have known that, themselves. Anyway this week J. comes in for lunch and tells me, Your friends are back from wherever they went.

Outside I don't see anybody. There are the usual swallowtails and wasps, and a gang of noisy crows that have invaded the turf covering our roof, but that's all. Then J. appears at my side and points to the lake.—Quack quack. Why don't you ask them where they've been?

I run the whole way there. There's more than last year, at least six or seven brown females and three males with white heads and green bars on their wings. I can't wait to see the babies that I know they'll be having.

Inside the house J. is scooping up chicken dumplings and poking his greasy finger at Gomer's delighted face. When I squat next to him he says, Proud of me?

—For what?

—For noticing them before you did.

—You're so clever, I say and kiss him. He kisses me back and the babies gurgle.—I have the smartest husband in the world.

—So you do and no mistake.

—All the others are jealous of me.

—Well I don't know about that, he laughs.—But they should be.

We finish eating fast and put the babies to sleep. It's a good thing they're all so little they don't mind taking naps. J. doesn't care, he'd stick his thing in me right in front of them, but it doesn't feel right with them there going naah naah and the twins waving and sucking on their toes.

Afterwards I let him sleep. Probably I should shake him and remind him of the barn he's building, but I don't. It's only spring and he's got a good start on it already. Every day he seems to get stronger and do more work.

I go outside and sit on a jumble of rocks by the lake. The sun's fallen halfway down the sky and a little breeze skips across the water. I hear our sheep bleating from some-where far off. Out in the center of the lake the ducks paddle around like they're waiting for something to happen.

Clouds speckle the sky like spots on an egg, but there's no storm coming that I can feel. For some reason I start thinking about the day we left Papa and Mama and the others. It was only about a year ago but it feels a lot longer. Sometimes I miss them *so much*, Ilya and Bera too and the time we spent in the tent getting ready. Other days I hardly think about them at all. It's kind of nice just being here with J. and all the animals, the ones for the farm and the ones J. calls my friends.

But still I remember that last morning and what Papa said. I've never asked J. about it because he'd tease me, but I don't really know what to make of it.—God reigns over everything, he said or I thought he did, and at the time I thought he was just talking the way he liked to. Saying Yahweh's in charge and you better be careful. But when we'd been traveling for a week we got caught in a storm, a bad one with lightning reaching across the sky like a praying mantis and thunder snapping behind every rock. J. and I got down among some boulders and stayed as dry as we could, which wasn't very. The animals all gathered around us with their heads down going moo baa snuffle and waited for it to pass. We did too.

J. leaned into me and yelled over the wind, We'll have a Hell of a story for the grandkids.

I smiled but didn't mean it much. It's something he says all the time now, but what's the point of telling a story if we can't even get it right?

I hardly remember Bera and Ilya talking about how they collected their animals. I should have asked them again but I forgot. Of course people will tell *some*thing, it was the end of the world after all. A story like that won't be forgotten. But things will get added and left out and confused, until in a little while people won't even know what's true and what's been made up.

The least we can do, J. and me, is get as much of it as right as we can. Which starts me wondering again, did Papa say

God reigns over everything

or did he say

God rains over everything

and does it matter?

Because I'm pretty sure it does. It seems like one of them says, God is in charge so *watch your step*. And the other says, God can take away everything but He'll *give back* everything too, so it's up to us what to make of the sun and rain and all the animals and whatever else we find. I think it matters which one we choose, because that's going to decide how we tell the story. When the story gets told, and told again and then *again*, things will change. They always do. Not on purpose, but just because people don't ever really *listen*.

So we should at least make sure we understand what happened to begin with.

When J. laughs behind me I look up and smile. He's got the twins in his arms, Magog reaching for me but Madai happy to chew on his father's hair.

My husband squats next to me and says, I've been calling your name. What're you thinking about so hard?

I shrug and point to the lake.—Where those ducks came from, I say.